THE ECHO DIES

Also by Roger Teichmann

DOG'S TWILIGHT

Nonfiction

LOGOS AND LIFE
(Anthem Press, 2022)

WITTGENSTEIN ON THOUGHT AND WILL
(Routledge, 2015)

NATURE, REASON AND THE GOOD LIFE
(OUP, 2011)

THE PHILOSOPHY OF ELIZABETH ANSCOMBE
(OUP, 2008)

THE CONCEPT OF TIME
(Macmillan, 1995)

ABSTRACT ENTITIES
(Macmillan, 1992)

THE ECHO DIES

ROGER TEICHMANN

AUTHOR'S NOTE

MUCH OF THE ACTION OF this novel takes place in the French town of Uzès, aptly dubbed by one of the characters 'the gem of Languedoc.' As real as the town itself are the dukes and duchesses of Uzès, the Crussol dynasty, although the duke to be met with in these pages, the unhappy Henri de Crussol, is a fiction. The village of Fournhac, also a fiction, nevertheless has for its model a certain village in the Creuse where a pub very like Les Pêcheurs may be found, overlooking a weir and probably still serving excellent steak frites.

I

I WILL HAVE ONE MORE Pernod, thought Julius as he let his gaze drift along the line of arches on the other side of the square, coming to rest on the central fountain. On the stone rim of the fountain perched a middle-aged couple, heads bent over a guidebook, backpacks sitting on the ground at their feet. I will have one more Pernod, thought Julius, then I will get up and wander round the town, reacquainting myself with its streets and alleys, its nooks, its vistas, its grand buildings and its shady corners. I will skirt the walls of the duke's chateau and crane my neck to gaze up at the Tour Fenestrelle.

He raised a hand and the young man waiting on the tables in that part of the square responded. With his other hand Julius held up his empty glass. The man nodded and turned away; the glass was a remote control, the waiter a puppet. Leaning back in his chair he stretched out, arms dangling at his sides, one foot upon its opposing ankle. Above him the leaves of a plane tree rustled in the breeze. It was late afternoon.

He'd touched down at Nîmes airport several hours earlier. Driving from Nîmes to Uzès through the smiling landscape he had set himself to reconstructing *Les Pêcheurs* in his imagination, the inn or pub which for years Maia had been running single-handed and where they were due to meet up in a couple of days. A poky two-story building with many windows at the confluence of three sleepy roads and overlooking a weir. Garden down to the river's edge. A stone bridge not far off, traversed by human beings, farm vehicles and the occasional car. On the other side of the river the town rose steeply and half way up the main road there was, if his memory served him, a small walled garden with a memorial stone honouring those local men and women who had fought in the Resistance, 1940-1945. Further up, the road levelling out, farm buildings began to appear, several in a state of picturesque abandonment. In the fields to either side, horses and cows. This was the little town of Fournhac, half an hour's drive from Uzès. Maia would welcome him into *Les Pêcheurs*, they would embrace and twenty years of absence would fall away.

'Come and see yourself exhibited,' she'd written on her postcard. 'Your portrait with mirror hangs between a Sun-and-Moon montage and Billy asleep on the sofa.' He assumed Billy was a cat, unless Maia had picked up a lover in the interim. The exhibition was to raise some money towards the upkeep of *Les Pêcheurs*; maybe business was slow. Julius planned to buy at least one piece.

The Pernod had arrived together with the customary slip of paper on a saucer. If I have a fourth Pernod he'll just have to print off another bill, thought Julius. He lifted the glass to his lips and felt something warm against his calf.

'You again.' He patted the dog's head. 'No more *biscotti* I'm afraid. You had my last.' The dog wagged its tail, happy to wait.

The breeze was getting up. In the plane trees the smaller branches swayed and someone's paper napkin slid and danced across the stones. A child's voice shouted 'Milou! Milou!' and the dog, electrified, performed a volte face and bounded off. Julius watched it run towards a little girl in the distance; she was bouncing a red ball up and down on the pavement, pam-pam, pam-pam. *Milou*... The memory of a film from the previous century came to him: *Milou en Mai*, about the 'events' of '68 when the turbulence of students and strikers threatened to bring down a government and shockwaves were felt even in the depths of rural France. Soundtrack by Stephane Grapelli with Marc Fosset. Director, Louis Malle.

My memory seems to be functioning all right, he thought, even if in that case the trigger was arbitrary. After all if I'd been asked 'What is the name of Louis Malle's film about *les événements*?' I'd have dried up. Or if you'd asked me 'What did you get Paul for his sixth birthday?' I'd have... He passed a hand across his brow. But we're dealing with all that. For the present, I'm to live *in* the present. I'm here on holiday to enjoy myself— to be charmed by this beautiful town, to take it easy, to meet up with an old friend, a dear old friend, to eat, drink and be merry ... A gust of wind picked up his bill and carried it off. He eyed it without concern. Up in the sky a plump little cloud, sharp-edged against the blue, was being pursued by its lumpier fellow. A bit early in the year for the mistral?

Julius reached inside his jacket pocket and brought out a leather wallet. (Toni gave me this.) His waiter was passing between tables bearing a tray with two beer bottles on it. (For my fortieth birthday.) Julius raised a hand—the waiter nodded and ignored him. On the other side of the square the little girl threw the ball with an impassioned gesture and Milou darted after it like a high-powered toy.

Compare and contrast. A dog acts because it cannot help it, its nature commands it. Milou is the slave of his passions, and his passions are open and simple. They function to keep him and the tribe of dogs in existence; even his fanatical devotion to the Master Race has that purpose. But in the heart of man there is sickness and dysfunction. We know the better and choose the worse. Or at any rate we fail to choose the better. For how many years have I been failing to maintain and nurture my love for my friends? It is a sin of omission. When, in my troubles, Maia held out her hand to save me from drowning, I swore I would return that token of love by tending the sacred flame of our friendship. And what have I done? I haven't visited, I haven't kept up a proper correspondence. I have been thoroughly inadequate. And her life has been hard, she has struggled, she has certainly struggled.

Julius sighed. The waiter was approaching, swinging his empty tray.

But the day after tomorrow we will embrace and she will forgive me.

'Oui, monsieur?'

'L'addition, s'il-vous plaît.'

The waiter looked at the little plate.

'It blew away,' explained Julius. The two men gave two independent shrugs and the waiter withdrew.

By now the breeze was definitely a wind. A fat man in a polo shirt and shorts walked past, his baseball cap held in place by pudgy fingers. People sitting at the café tables placed bottles and glasses on top of napkins. The rustling of leaves sounded like rushing water. Now the waiter was back; he stood over Julius while the latter extracted euros from a wallet and fumbled them into the young man's hand.

'Merci, monsieur.'

'Merci à vous.' Julius got to his feet. He felt a little dizzy, but nothing that couldn't be attributed to everyday causes. A walk in the wind would refresh him. Then he could return to the hotel and have a late siesta or pre-prandial nap as the case may be. (Mustn't forget to take that second pill.) Where to, then? The ducal palace, of course, a.k.a. duchy, a.k.a. chateau. He found himself hesitating as to which route to take: one could leave the Place aux Herbes by three or four different exits and his mind's eye was struggling to see round the corners of buildings to beat for itself a clear path to the duchy.

It was to the … to the south. To the north. No, to the north-east. It was …

Oh God. This is the problem, this is the shadow that falls over me. This is the trick my brain keeps playing on me. I know where it is, a moment ago I could have pointed towards the renowned duchy of Uzès without any difficulty, with my eyes closed. Well then, I'll close my eyes. Take a deep breath now, Julius, count to some number between ten and twenty, fifteen as it might be, and then slowly open your eyes, enjoy the lovely scene before you, and—and walk in *that* direction. Yes, over there, towards that building that juts into the square. That's right.

He was on track again, moving confidently across the square. The shadow had passed, the mechanism was operating smoothly.

*

The Rue Entre Les Tours conducts you in a roughly east-north-easterly direction away from the Place aux Herbes and towards the chateau of the dukes of Uzès. The dukes and duchesses of Uzès, rather. Julius had a soft spot for one duchess in particular, the one who achieved fame as the first woman driver in the country to be issued with a fine for speeding: 15 km per hour down the Bois de Boulogne in 1899. No such menace threatened pedestrians using the Rue Entre Les Tours. In fact there were no vehicles at all in the Street Between The Towers when Julius ambled along it, hands clasped behind his back and looking no doubt hopelessly English. The height of the buildings and the narrowness of the street seemed to be sheltering him from the mistral. They could have had the opposite effect of course, turning Between Towers Road into a tunnel or funnel. Or channel or runnel. Anyway, when he came out at the other end he would probably encounter it again.

One or two shops had popped up in the street since his last visit and he took in their wares with a semi-curious eye. The windows of a fancy patisserie and the neighbouring lingerie shop displayed their come-hither contents, seduction operating at different levels. Further on was a newsagent's with its rack of journals, amongst which Julius spotted *Le Monde* carrying a front-page story about 'le terrorisme'. The words of the President, apparently. He peered closer to establish which country's President. In the window of the newsagent's his double bent forward; the two parties straightened up smartly as if disconcerted by one another's proximity. Julius examined his reflection: a tall figure wearing a light linen jacket—bookish spectacles astride an aquiline, slightly crooked, nose—hair slicked back 'like the young Brahms' (as Maia had put it). Sixty-four, London academic and writer, divorcé, guinea pig for science. Well, not exactly—but Alethex was a new drug on the scene, as his GP had explained to him more than once when they sat opposite one another in a dingy windowless consulting room discussing his recent problems. As for sixty-four and the rest, that was all true. He strolled on, then remembered he hadn't determined the

President's nationality. French presumably, since it was the front page of *Le Monde*. He didn't go back to check.

This must be the fifth? sixth? time he'd visited Uzès, always staying in the same hotel, except one year when their plumbing had been in a bad way. Burst or bust pipes, and he couldn't now remember which sort of pipes. His alternative accommodation that year had been an Airbnb hovel two miles out of the city with ants in the kitchen and an insane dog next door. Since then his loyalty to the hotel had been complete. His first three visits took place in his twenties when his academic research first brought him over on the trail of Henri de Crussol, duc d'Uzès. Now here was a question: how had he ever got interested in the first place in that little-known but fascinating figure? Not only could he not remember the original stimulus, he couldn't remember whether he'd ever remembered what it was. But that was absurd; rather, he couldn't remember when it was he'd ceased to remember. Not that *that* sort of forgetfulness can be so unusual, surely? Can it?

He stood still. 'I don't know. I don't remember.'

It was comic, really. A comedy, a farce, in which the protagonist keeps doing double takes and looking for his keys several times in the same drawer. Then doesn't recognise himself in the mirror. Hilarious.

He passed his hand over his brow and walked on. Doubtless it was his supervisor who had first pointed him in the direction of H. de C. The history of the Huguenots was her thing and even if duke Henry wasn't himself a Huguenot there was plenty of that stuff going on in Uzès. Not to mention Nîmes. Yes, one can usually reconstruct the past, including one's own, on the basis of existing data and human probabilities. That was a principle of the historian's trade, after all. The historian is a detective, and so is the autobiographer, especially if he is losing . . .

Julius reeled under the impact of a pummelling blow. A gust of air hit him, and hit him again; he heard a shriek of alarm or delight a few yards away and looked to see a woman struggling with her skirt as with a live thing. The stock image of Marilyn Monroe above an air vent flitted before his mind. He grabbed a lamp post. Le mistral: le vent qui rend fou. 'The wind that makes you mad,' he said to himself and at the same time caught a glimpse of his face reflected in the shop window, grinning like a maniac.

*

Toni said, 'We should go on holiday somewhere. The three of us. Together.'

'Like where?'

'Like anywhere. I don't know—somewhere in Europe. Or Cuba. I've always wanted to visit Cuba.'

'Toni . . . the heat would be . . .'

'We don't have to go in the summer, do we.'

'What if he gets ill?'

'Cuba has one of the best health services in the world. Anyway, we can't just wrap him in cotton wool and go on as if . . .'

He put his hand on top of hers.

'Toni. Toni, darling. You heard what Dr Keller said; the next couple of months…'

She was shaking. He raised his hand to stroke her cheek.

They were sitting in The Bookworm, a café opposite the faculty, haunt of long-haired serious-looking humanities students. One of his own students was at a nearby table, her face lit up by the screen of her laptop, one hand wrapped round a disposable coffee cup.

*

When his marriage fell apart Maia had invited Julius to stay at Fournhac for as long as he wanted. He said goodbye forever to the flat in Manhattan, sent his meagre belongings across the ocean into storage somewhere in Oxford, and bought a one-way ticket from JFK to Nîmes. For six weeks he mourned, drank, talked to Maia into the small hours, felt that his life had come to an end, felt that his life was just beginning, wandered round the French countryside and slept. Especially he slept.

A job was waiting for him in Oxford. He'd been away for nine years and they were more than happy to have him back. It was the approved route: after being a graduate student, then a junior research fellow, one made oneself scarce, consolidating one's career in the process—at which point one could return. Some people planned it that way, but Julius hadn't. His American interlude was actually an aborted dream. A few of his more sympathetic colleagues even recognised this. Still, he threw himself into his work, and it was at that time that he began sketching out the book which was to make him (relatively speaking) famous. He could remember when the idea for it first struck him: he was standing on Broad Street watching a piece of masonry fall to the ground. Through an aperture in a hoarding could be seen a wrecker at work, demolishing a two-hundred-year-old building regarded by the authorities as surplus to requirements. Pasted on the hoarding was some fatuous message along the lines of 'Building a Better Future'. It didn't bother him at all that he couldn't remember the exact wording.

The book came out, and a few years later he was offered a chair at King's College, London. Once again he said goodbye to Oxford. This time it was adieu. KCL treated him well and he took to life in the metropolis more than he'd expected to. His lectures were popular and during the '20-22 pandemic, when remote pedagogy replaced live performance and Microsoft Teams supplanted the lecture hall, some of them filtered through—by accident and against protocol—to the wider world of the internet, enhancing further the fame that had come to him from *Pandora's Mirror*. He could probably have become a TV intellectual if he'd wanted to. Toni sent him a nice email congratulating him on the book. 'One day I hope to read it,' she wrote, as if she had no say in the matter.

Julius was vaguely reminded of the Broad St hoarding by a similar one stationed in the Place du Duché. No stirring message was pasted on it, it served simply to conceal some road works. But the blue was the same—another arbitrary trigger. He was leaning with his back against a wall for security against the mistral, which came in unpredictable gusts. Tall people have further to fall, he reasoned. Opposite him was the entrance to the duchy. An open wicket gate set within the main gate, itself set back from the road, afforded the inquisitive tourist a glimpse of the chateau within, sequestered behind whose shuttered windows must be whatever remained of an ancient family of French thoroughbreds. Its younger members no doubt spent most of the year in Paris or Monaco but surely a feisty and irascible chatelaine still stalked the dimly lit corridors of the palace? Or at least the head gardener could be heard discussing the football results with a liveried sous-chef? In reality the duchy now functioned mainly as a museum, despite the fact that the current duke was alive and well. Julius played with the idea of 'doing the tour' but decided against it. He could too easily imagine meeting with a series of improvements, such as an explanatory placard erected so as to obscure the thing it was explaining.

It was his own version of the duchy he was protecting, of course. When he was a budding historian of twenty-five his delight in pacing the same floors and seeing the same objects as Henri le Duc had been very sweet. Against the odds, the corny phrase beloved of guidebooks rang true: it really had been like stepping into the past. A past moreover that was colourful and bracing. Crenellations, spiral staircases, tapestries and high-backed chairs. 'Enter Errol Flynn handling his trusty rapier' was irreverent Toni's summing-up. He had smiled and shaken his head at her.

Across his field of vision, from right to left, moved the figure of a fat man in a polo shirt and shorts. His hand was still clamped to the baseball cap upon his head; Julius had the feeling that he had been conscientiously maintaining this pose for the last half hour, unless indeed he'd simply forgotten that he had put his hand there, like someone walking around with a napkin stuffed into his shirt front. But even as Julius gazed after him the hand lowered itself in a serene, deliberate movement. Was it a gesture of mockery? A playful goad? On the hastily unfolded piece of paper wrenched out of a packet of tablets: *Possible side-effects include paranoid delusions.* He hadn't read it but it might be there all the same. He would have to check. The packet was in a drawer by his bedside table. He saw himself pulling it out and fighting through cardboard to reach the flimsy document with its indications and contra-indications, its common and its merely rare side-effects (palpitations, nausea, death) . . .

No. These thoughts he would put away.

He opened the drawer and put them away.

*

Back in the hotel Julius flopped into an armchair and closed his eyes. He had asked at reception for a pot of tea accompanied by any nibbles the establishment might have to offer. 'Bit peckish.' 'I'm sorry?' The receptionist was a chic unsmiling woman in her twenties. Her command of English was good, Julius was surprised that 'peckish' had been a problem.

They'd installed three or four huge leather armchairs in the hotel lobby since his last visit, the sort you sink into so far you're never sure if you'll get out again. His knees were more or less at the level of his shoulders. Opening his eyes, he found them focusing on an artwork which hung on the wall opposite, a canvas splashed in primary colours, blandly cheerful. The sort of thing deemed suitable for lobbies, annexes and other public spaces. Hospitals. Madhouses.

As far as he knew Maia had never gone in for institutional art. Its breezy openness was alien to her; intimacy and depth were her modes. She might have done something for a church or convent, and indeed there was the one institution whose aims harmonised with hers, whose message might receive enhancement from her vision—not so surprising, given her early leanings. He wondered where she was on her spiritual path these days. (And he imagined her head tilting quizzically at the phrase.) Wherever or whatever it was it would be embodied in her painting.

Gliding towards him was his pot of tea, carried by a tall youth with a ponytail. The tray was placed before him on a low table and Julius was pleased to see olives, peanuts, even salami. Plus a saucer with a slip of paper on it.

'Merci beaucoup.'

'No problem,' replied the youth, and seeing the old man getting out his wallet: 'You needn't pay now, sir. That's just for your information. The amount will appear on your final bill.' He gave a seraphic smile.

'Ah yes,' said Julius, returning the wallet to its pocket. 'For my information. Thank you.' He reached for an olive.

'Is there anything else I can get you, sir?'

'No, this is fine.'

The youth beamed down at him.

'Thank you, sir.'

What for? thought Julius, watching the retreating ponytail. He tried some of the salami. Excellent. This should tide me over till dinnertime. And a nice pot of—he lifted the teapot lid—Darjeeling or something. Heaven-sent (yawn) refreshment. He rummaged among the peanuts.

A window was open somewhere and a delicious breeze made spasmodic incursions. The mistral had died down, for the time being at any rate. Did climate change have an effect on such things? He supposed so. The ice-cap had nearly gone, there were floods in Asia, plagues of locusts in Africa... It would be strange if the mistral got off scot free. The temperature in Uzès was certainly higher than he'd known it to be. And yet we keep on driving our cars, flying our planes and cutting down our rainforests. Kyoto was followed by Paris was followed by Glasgow. The ashes of the various Accords and Agreements drifted on the toxic air, and every day the cliff edge came a little closer.

And how did you travel yourself, Mr Durward? By aeroplane, was it? Hypocrite.

I am not a hypocrite, I am a follower of Immanuel Kant. If everyone flew as little as I fly, drove as little as I drive, built as few factories as I build or as I have in any way encouraged to be built, then we would be, if not all right, then a lot better off than we are. How else can one determine what's 'too much' or 'too little' than by specifying a rule of conduct such that universal adherence to that rule would result in the desired equilibrium?

Your plan would work splendidly, Mr Durward, if only you could persuade another eight billion or so people to adopt it.

It is not a 'plan', it is a criterion of rational behaviour.

The world doesn't need your 'criteria'—what it needs is action.

Philippe Arentz had uttered almost those exact words, sitting on a moth-eaten sofa in a Paris flat fifteen years ago. Philippe's hands shook—Julius never knew why—so that lighting a roll-up or flipping through the pages of a volume of Marcuse for a reference was always an ordeal; for Julius especially, as he waited for the answer to some question about *anomie* or the fragility of capitalism. On the morning when they first met a sunbeam cut through and illuminated the prodigious dust of the book-lined sanctuary, giving it the feel of a chapel. Stale cigarette smoke hung in the air like incense. Julius felt he was interviewing a Jesuit priest bodied forth as a Sorbonne radical with five o'clock shadow. There was the same dogma, the same calm certainty, the same misty-eyed eschatology—and coming like a refrain, the repeated call for 'action'. In the end, very little of the material garnered from those interviews made its way into *Pandora's Mirror*, but the soupçon of French radicalism lent a sharp tang to the whole. Other interviews with academics, though more fruitful, felt staid by comparison.

What is now being done by the oligarchs and bureaucrats of this country cries out to heaven for vengeance, or if heaven will not speak for us, the other place. That was the authentic voice of Philippe, echoing down the years. And there it was, with more of the same, emerging from the text of an email sent only a few weeks ago. Julius had rejoiced to receive it. Some things remain the same, he thought. In this world Philippe is a constant. A postscript to the email read: *If you're ever in France, get in touch. I'd like you to meet some friends of mine. They've all read your book.* Julius replied that he might well be visiting France later in the year, in which case he would of course be in touch, and how were Louise and the children? A second email from him informed Philippe of the dates of his holiday.

I wonder if he really wants to meet up. He never struck me as very sociable, his mind was too much on higher things for that. And yet he refers to 'some friends of mine'—by which I suppose he means 'fellow radicals'. If they've all read my book they're probably Philippe's own students, come to that. I never did properly check the French translation; odds on it's even more obscure than the original. What a tangled skein of thoughts it turned out to be. It certainly flummoxed the reviewers. People thought it must be profound, and perhaps it was. Whether it was or it wasn't, it did express some of the things that were on my mind at that time. You could say the book was a sort of catharsis; a catharsis and at the same time a reckoning. (He wondered if he wasn't subconsciously quoting an old review.) One thing was for sure, he couldn't perform a similar feat today. He'd been resting on his laurels for about a decade and very comfortable laurels they were, even if his employers had become twitchy about his failure to follow up. A couple of articles in rather obscure journals, that's all, not the sort of thing to add ballast to the department's research output, while any allowances made on the grounds of unfortunate personal circumstances had long since ceased to be legal tender.

He held an olive up between thumb and forefinger. In a few weeks, term would begin and he would be back in harness. He saw the rotund figure of his head of department bearing down on him and cornering him somewhere: 'How are you, Julius, did you have a *productive* summer?' Hugh was himself very productive. His own output had the healthy regularity of good bowel movements. Yet none of his writings had ever achieved the impact of *Pandora's Mirror*. So was his attitude to Julius motivated by a sense of departmental duty or by niggling envy? It was hard to say and the task wasn't made any easier by Hugh's robotic manner.

Julius yawned. Che sarà sarà. Meanwhile he had work to do. Work watering the precious plants of friendship. Maia. Phillipe. Uzès itself. Moreover, and of more immediate significance, in an hour's time dinner would be served. He extracted himself from the leather armchair's embrace, teetered a little, and moved off in the direction of the lift.

Room twenty-seven, second floor. Twin beds, en suite bathroom, view over a courtyard with yellow dustbins. Blissful familiarity. He got himself a glass of water from the bathroom, went over to the bedside table, pulled out the drawer and removed a blue packet from which he took a raft of pills. As he punctured it with the pad of his thumb he noticed his phone, which sat on top of a volume of Yeats, blinking at him. He swallowed an Alethex then picked up the phone. There were two emails waiting for him in his inbox.

The first was from Philippe: *Am staying with a friend in Nîmes. If you have wheels, come and visit. I can send you the address. Unless you'd prefer me to come to you. (Less convenient.) Amitiés, P.* Julius smiled. Philippe could come straight to the point when he was in the mood.

The other email was longer. He skimmed to the end to see who had sent it: Travis Beggs, PA to Harry D. Selkirk, Optimex Foundation. It seemed to be an invitation. His eye slipped to the second paragraph: *I would love to be able to talk this over with you at a venue of your choosing, perhaps over lunch? The Foundation would be happy to treat you on this occasion as an expression of our good will. Mr Selkirk has emphasized this in no uncertain terms. He is very keen to have you give the Inaugural Lecture, it would certainly be an honour for us. Speaking personally I would be thrilled to make your acquaintance . . .*

He thinks I'm in London—better let him know I'm in Uzès. What is the Optimex Foundation anyway? It must need inaugurating if they want an inaugural lecture. Then he read near the bottom of the email: *. . . a* *fee of £10,000.* Hiccup of surprise. Harry D. Selkirk must be a rich man to want to spend that sort of money on an hour's afflatus, however prestigious. Apparently he's very keen while his PA is on the verge of being thrilled. I must meet enthusiasm with enthusiasm I suppose, but not before Googling 'Optimex Foundation' and 'Harry D. Selkirk' to see if they're above board.

He imagined Hugh's reaction to hearing the news, and his reaction to Hugh's reaction: a mixture of complacency and relief. Yawning, he hoicked his feet up onto the bed, stretched out, closed his eyes and was asleep.

II

COLOUR OF A CLOUDLESS SKY, sky deep and pure, immanent living light, radiance of Our Lady, of Our Lady the colour of cloudless eyes, blue. This colour is our haven, this colour is the canopy above our heads. Into it we sink. Water and air.

Maia touched the canvas with her forefinger, left it there a moment. She withdrew the finger, stood back and tilted her head. Infinity of blue.

She was standing in a barn, dry earth underfoot. Around the walls of the barn paintings were hung: portraits, still lifes, stories, landscapes. The painting in front of her was an Annunciation. Mary stood perplexed, looking away from her unwelcome visitor, one hand distractedly fingering the pages of a book while the angel delivered his appalling message. The sky hung above and around them, distant and at the same time near.

The light in the barn was dim. Two windows, one without any panes, let in a modicum of sunshine, while a naked bulb hung from a central rafter and over in one corner was a standard lamp brought away from *Les*

Pêcheurs. The dim light suited the paintings on display, many of which spoke of things sensed not seen. A musty animal smell filled the air.

A local farmer, M. Bouvet, had allowed Maia the use of the barn in exchange for a vaguely proffered and as vaguely accepted promise of free refreshments at *Les Pêcheurs.* He had helped her carry the artwork from her old van, parked as close as she could get it, into the exhibition space; then he had left her to manage by herself. No chronological or even thematic ordering was evident in the arrangement of the paintings. Maia had simply put them where they seemed to want to go. Having hammered in nails at roughly equal intervals, she hung a ploughed field next to an abstract swirl next to a charcoal nude (Johnny after a bath). Then she stood back to take in the ensemble, and if something didn't look right two pieces could be swapped around. That was generally all it needed.

She passed from the Annunciation to its neighbour. A large ginger cat sprawled on a blue sofa, his half-closed eyes probably registering more than they appeared to. Dear old Billy, may he rest in peace. She had been his companion from kittenhood to doddery old age. Upon the life of a cat a human being looks down as from an Olympian height, perceiving the whole and what lies to either side of it. With the life of a fellow human being one's own is enmeshed, is on a level, is necessarily contiguous. She turned to the next painting, of a gaunt man seated on a kitchen chair, legs crossed, hands resting one atop the other on his knee, face partly in shadow. He was wearing jeans, a brown corduroy jacket and a green cravat; behind him a circular mirror hung upon the wall in which one could see the back of his head reflected. It was Julius aged thirty-ish, before he wore glasses and before his troubles began. Maia interrogated the painted face: How has life treated you? What new contours has it moulded? The idea occurred to her of painting him a second time, of capturing the same soul in flight further along its journey. She hadn't stayed still herself in the interim: side by side the two paintings would reveal a double journey.

He would be in Fournhac tomorrow. She saw him walking towards her, a shy smile on his face and nodding with pleasure. Enmeshed, contiguous with her, even when—and for how long!—absent from her. She felt a pang of guilt at the recollection that a bookmark in her copy of *Pandora's Mirror* had never travelled beyond page 23. Julius, I prefer your conversation. It's as Socrates said—if you ask a book a question, it can only repeat back at you what it's already told you. I want to hear the sound of your voice. And I will, tomorrow.

There was a rustle and a knock, two timid taps on wood. 'Excusez-moi, madame.'

Maia turned round. A girl of about eight and a boy a couple of years younger stood in the doorway, children of M. Bouvet.

'Maman... My mother, she has—she says, Can we help you?' The girl spoke, olive-skinned and dark.

'Help me? That's kind... Let me think.' Maia looked up into the rafters considering, then 'Yes, I think you can help me,' and she went over to an old rucksack sitting on the ground, reached inside it and brought out a sheaf of A4 leaflets. One of them slipped from her hand and floated zig-zag to the floor. She bent over to pick it up. 'You can put these in neat piles on that table over there.'

The girl came forward with outstretched hands; the boy hung back at first, then with the purposefulness of a sleepwalker followed in his sister's wake as she moved with her load towards the table. She has good English, thought Maia. Her parents and her school know that it's the universal language, the lingua franca. Perhaps she'll become effectively bilingual, then she can choose where to live, as I chose where to live by following Johnny to this little town, dreams in our heads and silly innocence in our hearts. Not that either of us was bilingual.

Choosing where to live: wasn't that just another case of putting oneself in God's hands, of jumping into the stream with eyes closed?

Yes. That is what choice is.

She looked at her watch. Eleven forty-five. She would need to get back to the pub soon. Things were pretty well set up in the barn, now it was simply down to her friends and customers to turn up. Doors open at 6 p.m. and the exhibition lasts a week. Let me give you a leaflet, Monsieur X, Madame Y. You will find much to interest and amuse you.

'Thank you, children. Merci, les enfants.'

She began gathering up her things and the children understood that they were being dismissed. A moment later they had disappeared. Outside the barn their receding voices, uninhibited by an adult presence, broke into a chirruping that was soon punctuated by the barking of a dog. Maia checked the innards of her rucksack, switched off the lights and went out of the building and into the sunshine.

Her van stood on the side of the road, separated from her by a shallow brook running down the length of the field. There was a narrow footbridge with a single wooden handrail. It was as easy for a sure-footed person to jump over the stream, but Maia was not a sure-footed person so she made use of the bridge, fingertips touching the handrail more for luck than for support. She reached the other side and—oh … something pungent … She quickened her step. The van, its offside front window open, was parked in the full glare of the morning sun and sitting in a shopping bag on the passenger seat wedged between other items from the Ecomarché was a Camembert which would be approaching liquidity. *You're going to leave all those paintings in an unlocked barn where anyone can steal them?* she heard her mother's voice demanding. Yes, mother—though you are not my mother—I am. I trust my neighbours, since trusting is a part of love and we are commanded to love our neighbour. And what would farmer Bouvet or Madame Moreau from the post office want with one of my paintings in any case? *Then why do you think they'll pay for them just because they're being exhibited?* But the voice was retreating, was submerging itself in the revving of the van's engine, as she had taught it to do.

About half way down the hill, just past the memorial garden, was a newsagent's. Maia pulled up in front of it. She preferred her news to be printed rather than on-line, partly because of the unreliability of her internet connection and partly out of an attachment to regional newspapers with their coverage of all things low-key and mundane—cattle shows, church fêtes, or on an exciting day a couple of youths getting arrested for joy-riding. But today she wished to know about more serious matters. The protests across France had been intensifying. These were largely, though not solely, concerned with climate change and the environment, and one target among others was the proposal to build a high-security 'research centre' in the middle of the Languedoc forests not far from Fournhac. The idea of it made her blood run cold. Dear Lord, who gave to Man custody over the earth and over living things, see how he abuses his charge; how he lays waste merely that he might enhance his powers.

The newsagent's was actually a general store, selling chocolates, light bulbs, loo paper, flowers and other miscellanea as well as newspapers and magazines. Remembering Julius's partiality to candles Maia picked up a box of matches, took down a copy of a national newspaper from the display rack and presented them at the counter.

'Bonjour, Madame.'

In thirty years M. Carnet, cheerfully obese and smelling of cigarettes, had never varied his greeting, never in fact called her by her name. Maybe its foreignness was a hurdle. In any case their relationship was perfectly cordial.

'Bonjour, Monsieur Carnet.'

He received her money and returned her change, all the time continuing to look out of the window into the street where nothing was happening. On the front page of the paper she brought back with her to the van was a photograph of a middle-aged man above the caption *DISPARU*. I'll read it later, she thought. There might be news about the protests inside.

*

Among the regular clientele of *Les Pêcheurs* was Brian Decker, known in those parts as the unofficial 'agent' for British owners of nearby holiday gites. He kept an eye on the properties and looked after the keys, which he would secrete under a flower pot or on a specified ledge in advance of the arrival of holidaymakers from the UK. (Somebody else will have made the beds and replenished the coffee.) These ancient customs had survived the trauma of Brexit, if trauma was the word, and Brian himself continued happily in his role as local expat, having years ago made enough money in the City to retire with his wife to the proverbial cottage with roses round the door a few miles out of Fournhac.

'Embarras de choix, as usual,' he commented, sitting on a barstool. His eyes moved from line to line of a menu chalked on a blackboard behind the bar: Moules Marinières, Steak Frites, Crêpe au Fromage de Chèvre . . . A gin and tonic sat by his elbow.

'How's Catherine?' asked Maia.

'Steak frites for me. Steak and gin, the wages of sin.' He downed his G & T and wiped a neatly-clipped moustache. 'Catherine's all right, thank you. Looking forward to your exhibition. As am I of course. Didn't know you could paint. Is that thing yours?'

He waggled a finger in the direction of a small oil painting hung above the low doorway of the pub and by this arcane gesture apparently caused the door to open. A stooping figure dressed in overalls came in.

'Bonjour,' called out Maia.

Seating himself next to Brian the man grunted and said, 'Everywhere the English. I will have to pray to Jeanne d'Arc.'

'You'd better sort out your football team first,' said Brian.

'Some wine, George?' asked Maia, reaching for a glass.

'S'il vous plaît. A nice glass of wine, if you please.' He pronounced the words with mincing precision.

'You're right, it sounds hopeless in English,' said Brian. 'In your English, I mean.'

Maia left them to it, going through the door into the corridor that led to the kitchen. Here she gave the order for Brian's steak frites to Béatrice, a new member of staff who she was training up. Béatrice was the third new employee in as many months. In the old days Maia would have taken such things in her stride but now she merely felt tired. Oh Johnny, I feel tired. Can you see how tired I feel? When we were young it was all an adventure, the obstacles themselves were our playfellows. We got up in the morning and went out to meet the world together shoulder to shoulder. Do your worst, world! If the rain came through the roof or the van wouldn't start or your bank refused you another loan, what did that matter when each day ended with your brown eyes smiling, a bottle of wine between us on the table, the warmth of your body in my bed? And now some other woman's bed enjoys that warmth and I don't even know her name. I don't even know where you're living, whether it's in France or some other country, maybe you've gone back to Ireland Johnny, Johnny I don't even know if you're still alive.

But all shall be well, and all shall be well, and all manner of things shall be well. And Béatrice may end up liking it here.

Maia left the kitchen and returned to the bar.

'…floating head down in the water. Seemed to be caught up in the reeds by the bank, he said. Near the old mill, where the river narrows.'

'Did anyone else see it?'

'No, I don't think so, and Patrice, who was fishing all morning not far down from there, says he thinks it's a load of nonsense. Thinks the old man must have been tipsy.'

A third had joined them, Dave Gibbard, another expat, full-jowled and bearded à la Hemingway. *Les Pêcheurs* had long ago established itself as a magnet for local Brits, as soon as it became known that the new landlord was Irish and his lady wife English. Their French neighbours didn't appear to mind, despite all George's quips.

'What's all this?' Maia asked.

'A beer, please,' began Dave. 'Old Vincent, you know, Vincent who used to run the riding school, he was down by the river—thanks—by the river this morning, and says he saw a body floating head down near the bank, stuck in ...'

'Why did Vincent not then telephone the police?' put in George. 'He is more keen to tell a story than to solve a crime, that is why.'

'If there's been a crime,' added Brian.

'C'est ça,' concluded George.

'Shouldn't someone go and investigate?' said Maia.

'Do you remember,' Brian said, 'when that big house at the top of the Rue Faventines, the one that used to be a hotel, started giving off bloody awful smells and someone got the police in, thinking it was dead bodies? And the police broke in and it turned out to be a fridgeful of fish? The owners had gone on holiday without paying their electricity bills ...' He chuckled. 'Bloody awful smell it was, you didn't want to be downwind of that, I can tell you.'

'Yes, the police, they are busy enough as it is,' said George, 'especially with all the climate protests that occur now; in a week or two I think Paris will be standing still.'

'At a standstill,' suggested Dave.

'C'est ça. They are threatening this and threatening that, marching down the Champs Elysées, it will be barricades and—and ... bombes à essence, how do you say that?'

'Molotov cocktails,' said Brian. 'In 1968 the students used cobbles off the streets to hurl at the police. There's ingenuity. Afterwards the authorities tarmacked over those bits so they couldn't do it again.'

'During the next round of disturbances,' finished Dave.

'The French, eh?' said George, leaning forward on his stool, bushy eyebrows hoisted. 'Always some bee in their bonnet.' (He enjoyed drawing on his stock of English idioms.)

'Remember the gilets jaunes?' said Dave.

'Lots of angry farmers . . .' said Brian.

George raised his glass and threw back his head. 'Vive la Révolution!' he thundered. Someone at the other end of the room clapped. George bowed in acknowledgement and slid his empty glass in Maia's direction.

Dave was reading the front page of the newspaper Maia had bought that morning and which had been lying neglected on the bar. He unfolded it for a fuller view. After a while he began scratching his beard. 'Says here . . .' He read a few more lines. Dave's French was adequate but he wanted to make sure he had the story. 'Says here that that expert who was submitting evidence to the committee of enquiry on the virology institute, the one they want to build over near Valliguières—he's gone missing. Five days ago.'

George emitted a low whistle.

'Any other details?' asked Brian.

'Not much. His family say he was fine. In good spirits.'

Maia crossed herself.

'Steak frites?' Béatrice, aproned and perspiring, stood among them holding a plate.

'An angel from heaven!' Brian waggled a finger by way of self-indication. The plate was put before him followed by a knife and fork wrapped in a paper napkin. Béatrice made her exit. I hope she settles in, thought Maia.

*

Maia first met Johnny through Julius. It was when she was still a postulant, putting her vocation to the test and asking God, 'Is it me you want? Is it me?'—craning inwardly to hear the answer, which sometimes she thought she heard, muffled, like a cry borne on the wind, borne away from her, a Yes or a No. Or just the wind in the trees.

Then Johnny had stepped into her life, larger than life and louder than the voice on the wind. Much louder, drowning out the voice and the other voices in her head as well, and saying, '*This* is real.' What a gust, what a tidal wave of reality! It, he, knocked her over, and for a while she lay sprawling, for a few weeks she sprawled on the ground, at the end of which God released her. Or she released God—stopped pestering Him with her 'Is it I?'

Johnny was a layabout and musician, working at that time as a gardener in one of the colleges. Julius had met him at a party, got to know him a bit, and on the strength of Maia's love of music had effected an introduction. It was fairly clear to all three that he was trying to set them up, or at any rate bringing them together with a chemist's curiosity to see what ensued—fireworks, a noxious gas, some harmless bubbles. It didn't escape Maia what this might imply as regards Julius's estimate of her religious impulse. She felt only mildly aggrieved and the whole thing eventually became a running joke between them: Venus v. Virtue—Mother Church v. the flesh the world and the devil. During this time, she now perceived, she simply put her relationship with God on hold. Her faith hibernated.

Johnny was a few years older than Maia and Julius: twenty-eight to their twenty-four. 'Pushing thirty, nearly over the hill,' he would say to her sadly as if warning her. He knew she wouldn't heed a warning like that of course, not even if he'd been forty-eight or fifty-eight: such was his self-confidence, the self-confidence of one blessed with obvious good looks and plenty of animal vitality. I must be so *simple*, reflected Maia. At first the three of them would meet together, cycle around the lanes of Oxfordshire together, go to concerts together. Huddled intimacy up in the top seats of the Sheldonian Theatre . . . tactile, electric, never to be forgotten. The orchestra played Bruckner and Maia felt she might faint. Then after a few months the gravitational attraction between Maia and Johnny threw Julius into orbit, until he spun off into space and they were alone together. Except that it had been they who had spun off leaving Julius alone—alone with his books and his research, his hankering after the past, a hankering that took him across the channel to France and Uzès, home of his beloved duke Henry. Johnny and Maia had visited him there and it must have been on that trip that Johnny hatched the idea of purchasing a little place, a little business proposition, in idyllic Languedoc. He bought the place first then asked her if she'd join him, confident of her reply. Incorrigible self-confidence. No wonder she'd been unable to keep a hold of him.

'This would look nice behind the bar, don't you think?'

Maia pointed at a cage with a stuffed bird in it. They were standing amid rickety chairs, stone flagons, old prints, walking sticks, typewriters, hats, horse tack, flails—the flotsam of generations of anonymous farmers, bourgeoisie and country gentlefolk.

'Does it sing?' replied Johnny.

She punched him softly. 'Well, I like it.'

'Add it to the list. What about that martingale?'

'Looks like bondage gear.'

'Now there's a thought…'

'No way, José. That little oil painting, the one of sunflowers…' She took it down for a closer look. The proprietor hovered in the background.

Shopping for bric à brac: up there with sunset strolls and helpless laughter. And sex. Maia found to her surprise that she had a talent for all these things, but it was the memories of shopping for bric à brac that came back to haunt her in the bleak days after Johnny's departure. It was the nesting instinct of course, nothing more. (But why not say, nothing *less*?) The pub was to be their nest, their home, their palace; naturally it had to be filled with objects singing and exclaiming, 'Johnny and Maia chose us!' If the things were quirky or absurd, well, what could be more suitable for a pub aesthetic, at least according to British standards? And some of them really were beautiful—the sunflowers, for example.

'Where do you want me to hang this, pops?'

'Why not above the doorway?'

Johnny placed the painting on a window sill and dragged a stool over to the door. Once up on the stool he banged a nail into the wall. Then she handed him the painting. Their eyes met and he said 'I love you.'

Yes, he did love me. This is a fact that cannot be erased. I must be grateful for it as I am for the sunflowers and for the blue of the sky. It is better to have loved and lost than never to have loved at all says the poet, but the taint of self can be heard in that utterance, for he is consoling himself with a calculation: Love-pleasure minus Loss-pain > Default state. To have been loved is a gift just as much as is being now loved, or as is that future state of belovedness which has been promised us. Past love is as real as present or future love. And all such gifts are gratuitous and undeserved; calculation plays no role in the heart's reception of them, gratitude alone shall be the song upon my lips.

'Vingt euros,' said the proprietor, and Johnny reached into his pocket.

'What about my caged bird?' asked Maia with mock plaintiveness.

'We can always come back for it.' He gave her a peck on the cheek. 'I don't think people will be queuing up to buy it.'

*

She had a couple of hours before the barn doors opened and the exhibition began. Who would show up? The Deckers, surely… maybe… and M. and Mme. Bouvet with their children. George. Patrice with his girlfriend. And which paintings would be most popular? Would the depictions of Fournhac and the surrounding countryside appeal to that love of the familiar natural to people whose ancestors lay side by side in the walled suburb or annexe nestling on the edge of the town which was the cemetery? Or would her two self-portraits jump out at them, inducing a turning of the head from canvas to human subject and back again, a savouring of the differences as much as the likenesses, an unspoken verdict, 'She looks better in the flesh / in the painting'? Her frizzy hair, now grey, appeared rejuvenated and black in the earlier self-portrait—but it was no less abundant now than it had been then, nor would she ever prune and cut back what Johnny had once so admired.

She had to remind herself that the paintings were for sale, most of them. That the purpose of the exhibition was to earn money, not garner praise. It would be hard to part with them, a little hard anyway… and of course they were unlikely to travel very far. She would probably encounter them again on neighbourly visits, in living rooms and kitchens.

I will go for a walk, she thought. I will clear my mind.

The three roads leading away from *Les Pêcheurs* offered three different experiences: one took you past stables and the remnants of the old riding school, with fields and hills to your right—another wound through a neighbourhood of newish houses until you reached the abrupt limit of the town, beyond which lay the open road—while by the third route you found yourself walking along an avenue of poplars from which at a certain point you could descend to the river, to follow its dreamy course for as long as you wished. (Or you could eschew the avenue of poplars and cross the bridge into town, proceeding if you felt like it all the way up to M. Bouvet's farm. But that wasn't a 'walk'.) Johnny had preferred the walk past the stables. The sight of horses always aroused him; 'It's my Irish blood,' he would explain. Sometimes Maia would take that route for his sake, confessing and permitting to herself the foolish glimmering hope—that she might come across him leaning casually on a fence, his beautiful profile turned towards her ... watching the horses. But her own preference had always been for the riverside walk. Now she made for the avenue of poplars. To walk between the slender columns with their leaves whispering above her head was like participating in a ceremony, as bride or pilgrim or Vestal virgin. Sometimes she felt as if a benign force were drawing her down the avenue: surely her feet moved spontaneously? Her mother would call this wool-gathering. But (or therefore) she allowed herself to yield to it. It was the spirit of the trees entering into her, it was the light and the air and the earthsmells all pervading, all undoing, untying the knots, the tangle of Self. Dappled sunlight fell on the ground as a carpet under her feet. The sound of rushing water came to her from the weir. Dear Lord ...

How easy it was to pray in these surroundings! One's body seemed to be praying just by moving through space, by encountering the earth underfoot and feeling the warmth on one's skin. She turned out of the avenue down a grass slope and towards the river. Soon she was standing by the river's edge. The water moved slowly, its sluggish journey taking it from somewhere to somewhere; on the bank opposite sat a duck and a drake, somnolent in the sun, plain and gaudy respectively. *Male and female created He them.* And the rest is history, as Julius might have said.

She strolled along the path by the bank of the river and hummed softly to herself. Midges danced in the air around her. The trees became thicker on each side of the river as you progressed, and round the next bend she would be able to see the old water mill. High above her a lone buzzard communed with the void, describing a vast circle over the land.

Her back trouser pocket hummed and vibrated; it was her phone. She retrieved it: 'Oui, allo, Maia Byrne.'

'Maia.'

'Julius…'

She stopped. The midges danced.

'Your voice—'

'You recognised me at once. Dear Maia, I'm flattered.'

'Oh Julius, you're here!'

'Of course I am. Well, *here* actually. And you're there.' She laughed.

'Have I taken you by surprise?'

'No, no… not at all. Julius, how lovely to hear your voice! I'm walking by the river, you remember the river? You used to stand on the bridge—'

'The stone bridge—'

'Yes—'

'—which takes you into town and up the hill. I remember everything, Maia. Everything.'

'And you'll be here tomorrow? You're not ringing to say you can't come?'

'No, silly, I'm ringing to say I *can* come. Will come. Tomorrow, as you know—probably mid-afternoon, around four. I'm seeing an old friend in Nîmes in the morning, then I can come straight to you after lunch.'

The illusion of his physical presence was overpowering. Maia walked along the river path feeling light, almost weightless. She said: 'I've prepared the guest room for you. Some geraniums by your bedside, a sprig of lavender on your pillow.'

'Bible on the lectern…'

'Bien sûr. Open at the story of the Prodigal Son. And I bought a Camembert.'

'Sacre bleu! The crème de la crème, fromage du fromage rather.'

'You've hired a car?'

'Bien sûr. And I'm staying in my old haunt here. Had a Pernod in the Place aux Herbes yesterday, almost got blown over by the mistral. It was just like the old days. And I met a dog called Milou.'

'He introduced himself?'

'Not quite, but he obviously wanted to. Maia, do you remember that film by Louis Malle? ...'

She had gone past the bend in the river and ahead of her was the overgrown windowless water mill, its huge millwheel still in place, birds nesting in the brickwork. Around it grew oaks and willows; where it met the water a mass of rushes came up to meet it.

' ... staying down in the country when the shit hit the fan—May 1968, all that stuff. Very good film, I recommend it. He also directed *Au Revoir, Les Enfants*. Anyway, I'm just babbling, tell me about your exhibition, is it up and running? How many paintings are you showing?'

'It starts in an hour or so. About twenty. Nearly forty years' worth, Julius, can you believe it ...'

Amid the rushes a curlew stood looking out at her. It was perched on a stone that stuck out of the water. Suddenly the bird spread its wings and flew off into the woods; the stone bobbed up and down. But it wasn't a stone. It was the sole of a shoe, and beyond it, just visible among the reeds, was a trousered leg.

III

HE HAD BEEN ON A long, long journey, walking for days on end—coming from he couldn't remember where and going towards he didn't know what, footsore now and weary. It was night, the sky bristled with stars. He came to a low wall or parapet and looked over it down into an orchard. The trees stood in neat rows, bathed in a dim light, mysterious and expectant. Scented breezes cooled his tear-stained cheeks and as he turned his head towards the sky he heard a child's voice calling to him from far away. Out of the star-filled canopy a curved segment had been cut: an arch of deeper darkness against the dark velvet of the sky. The child's voice called again and the black arch shrank to a point and the stars rushed in.

Julius woke to find his duvet half way off the bed. He pulled it back. Where am I? Hotel Jaurès, Uzès. You have stayed two ... no, three nights. Sunlight penetrated the flimsy curtains of his room and he judged it to be about 8 a.m. It came back to him that he would be driving to Nîmes after breakfast, and after lunch from Nîmes on to Fournhac. Time to get moving. The dream-aura hung about him and he knew that to close his eyes would be to succumb to it. With a grunt he heaved himself out of bed and made for the bathroom. Defecation, ablution, accoutrement—the morning protocol, saved from tedium by the feeling of being on holiday, as embodied in novel light fixtures, tea-making equipment, complimentary biscuits, an unused remote control by the bed, and in a moment the welcome deluge of a power shower. Spruced and refreshed he would sally forth (not forgetting his room key) to take the lift down to the breakfast room.

Half an hour later Julius stood plate in hand before the cold cuts, cheese, cereals, yoghurt, fruit and croissants. As always he found he could only face croissants. He plied the tongs with his free hand. Two or three couples were already down for breakfast and the murmur of sotto voce conversation blended with piped music so nearly inaudible as to be innocuous. Back at his table he sipped the froth of his cappuccino and freed two delicate knobs of butter from their miniature envelopes. The ponytailed youth moved around in attendance on the company. 'Bonjour,' Julius offered when he came within earshot. 'Good morning, sir,' came the sunny reply.

A copy of yesterday's newspaper lay discarded on an adjacent table. The photo on its front page caught his eye: unsmiling mugshot of missing person. An old clerihew bubbled up from the depths of his memory:

If I had been
Albertine,
I'd have disparue
Too.

Albertine Disparue, nth volume of Proust's great opus, rendered by Scott Moncrieff as *The Sweet Cheat Gone.* He chewed on a croissant and nodded with satisfaction. One day he would read Proust all the way through.

'Anything planned today, sir?'

Julius looked up. 'Today? Yes—yes, I'm seeing a friend in Nîmes. He's…'

'Nîmes is a lovely city, sir, you'll have a great time. So much to see.' Radiant smile.

'Yes,' agreed Julius.

The young man inclined his head in an *Amen* and moved off. A pair of stout middle-aged women came into the breakfast room and stood for a few seconds assessing the situation. Conventionally if disappointingly two middle-aged men arrived to join them. The coffee was more lukewarm than hot and it wasn't long before Julius had consumed it and the croissants. He was about to get up when a familiar doubt took hold of him: had he taken his morning Alethex? Surely yes—with the usual bedside glass of water, head tilted back to help the little yellow pill on its way down his gullet. And yet… no verifying image of blue packet, empty glass, view of the ceiling, came to his assistance. His mind's eye drew a blank. Could he rely solely on the regularity of this habit, a habit he had only adopted a few weeks earlier? He was an old dog, it was a new trick. 'Bugger,' he muttered aloud, screwing up his napkin. If he returned to his room there would be tell-tale signs. He got up and made his way to the lift.

But once he was in his room he realised he didn't know what tell-tale signs to look for. He didn't know what tale was being told by the signs that he did find there, or whether any tale was being told, or if they were signs.

*

The road from Nîmes to Uzès, and from Uzès to Nîmes, is the D979. Beautiful countryside lies to either side of it and Julius's mood lightened as he drove. From the car radio came the life-affirming sounds of a Haydn string quartet. In his old Volkswagen back at home it would be a choice between music and air conditioning but the AC in this slick new hire car was as good as noiseless.

Philippe had sent him the address of a house some-where in the outskirts of Nîmes, along with a set of me-ticulous directions. He hoped that his route would take him past at least one of Nîmes' Roman buildings; if not, he might insist that they take a walk in the city centre, for the good of body and soul. In the first century B.C. Julius Caesar rewarded veterans of his Egyptian cam-paigns with plots of land to cultivate in the Gaulish plains and out of the efforts of those battle-scarred ex-pats sprang the town of Nemausus. The amphitheatre, a younger brother of the Coliseum in Rome, would later be used for bullfights, while the temple known as the Maison Carée so impressed founding father and amateur architect Thomas Jefferson that he based his design for the Virginia State Capitol on it. Then of course there was the aqueduct.

What geniuses they were, the Romans. *Genius*: itself a Roman word, like so many others in English (and French and Italian and Spanish and Rumanian…). Aqueducts, language, law courts—what *didn't* they bequeath to us, and wasn't Jefferson right to want his nascent American republic to share the trappings, and not just the trappings but also the spirit (the genius), of ancient Rome? Julius Caesar himself, my namesake, though he ended up stabbed to death on the steps of the Curia like some mafia don—doesn't he represent for us an ideal? A model? Courage and nobility. Intelligence and ambition.

On the other hand, tyranny and pride. In the end it was tyranny, or perceived tyranny, that did for him. One advantage of autocracy is that the remedy for tyranny is simple: kill the tyrant. Cut off the head. And there'll only be one head, ex hypothesi, unlike the case in which a group—small or large, politburo or populace—descends into tyranny. It's harder to bump off a whole cabinet, though it's been tried, and as for the People, you can hardly eliminate and replace it. You can pre-empt its wrath with education, cheap holidays, bread and circuses, but when it does get infected with mob frenzy you'd better just stay indoors, or alternatively cultivate your garden as Rousseau advised. I mean Voltaire.

That's why anarchism is so naïve. Tears of justified rage blind the anarchist's eyes to all the evidence of dark irrational forces lying pent up in the hearts of ordinary well-behaved folks, forces which if released will set them off on orgies of violence and destruction. True, it's usually a few far-sighted individuals who provoke the People into action, leaders and demagogues who one day (surprise, surprise!) set themselves up as the People's rulers, and so bring order and prosperity. And tyranny and pride and the Ides of March. Ladies and gentlemen, behold the whirligig of history.

He was rehearsing his old debates with Philippe, of course. Philippe was, or had been, a self-styled anarchist. Even allowing for the 'creative' use of words so characteristic of the academy, especially the French academy, Julius regarded this badge worn by his friend as a little vulgar, a little jejune. 'Don't you just mean *social critic*?' he would ask. 'I mean what I say,' Philippe would reply. 'Go on,' invited Julius, and Arentz the Anarchist took the stand: 'I reject the straitjacket of laws binding and suffocating the body politic.' Or words to that effect. Foucauldian frippery.

The Haydn had changed without his noticing it to Edith Piaf. Elle ne regrette rien. Julius hummed along to the whisky-sodden tune. Ahead of him he saw a sign for an exit onto a roadside stopping-place or aire de repos—an opportunity to stretch his legs and have a discreet pee behind a bush. He turned off the D979 and found himself pulling up by a meadow of wildflowers overlooked by a solitary picnic bench. Still humming, he got out of the car. The warm air hugged him close as he walked towards the meadow, an undulating patchwork of colours.

But he could hardly wade in among the flowers to do his business; wasn't there a tree or something somewhere? He looked back to the road. There wasn't much traffic—about a vehicle a minute, he guessed. Might as well piss al fresco.

He had just unzipped his flies when a muffled tintinnabulation started up. He paused pre-stream to interpret the sound, then putting himself on hold and cursing hurried back to the car. His phone was buried beneath a jumper and a road map.

'Hello? Philippe?'

An unfamiliar voice with a North American twang answered. 'Professor Durward?'

Julius frowned. Who the hell ...

'This is Julius Durward speaking.'

'Hello, Professor Durward, it's Travis Beggs. I thought I would just check in.'

'Travis ...' Oh God. The man from Optimex. I said I would see him today. In an email, an email I wrote just twenty-four hours ago. Having already arranged to see Philippe, then Maia, then ...

'Are you in Uzès?'

'No, we've—I've just got into Nîmes. I'm still on the plane, actually.'

Julius saw the crush of bodies, people pulling luggage out of overhead lockers while others struggled, stooping, out of their window seats and still others, like Travis Beggs, talked on their phones to invisible interlocutors.

'Ah. Mr Beggs. Thank you for getting in touch. I'm afraid I'm not in Uzès myself right now. I've been called away—on business . . .'

'Don't worry, Professor Durward, I completely understand.' Pause. 'May I ask, will you be returning to Uzès?'

'Oh yes, of course! Yes, no—I'll just be away a couple of nights, back on—whenever it is . . . You see, I have to go to Nîmes to see a, yes Nîmes, where you've just touched down, that makes it worse really, doesn't it. I'm so sorry, I've been rather disorganised. I guess I need a secretary.'

Longer pause. 'Sorry, professor, you broke up a bit there . . . maybe when the . . . on Friday if that . . . I do . . . -ation.'

The line went dead.

Maybe when the on Friday if that I do ation. If there is a mental Law of Entropy, our thoughts are tending to just such a state of irreversible disorder, flashes of apparent sense amid a stream of gobbledygook. He looked for comfort over to the wildflower meadow. Reds, blues and yellows were joined in harmonious chorus; order and beauty had emerged out of randomness . . . A text came through from Travis Beggs. Julius read it, deliberated, and sent off a reply. Okay, I mustn't forget: Friday at 2 p.m. in the hotel lobby. He took a pen from his shirt pocket and wrote down the details on the back of his hand.

A blue Fiat had come off the D979 and was pulling up behind his Peugeot. It came to a halt and a woman and a small boy got out. Papa remained at the wheel, dangling a smoking cigarette out of his open window. 'Voilà,' sang the woman, guiding her offspring towards the wildflowers. In a moment the boy's shorts were round his ankles and he was pissing happily among the stalks. Julius realised he had missed his chance; also, that his flies were undone. Nonchalantly he pulled open the car door as a shield, although the woman's attention was absorbed by her son's performance. Julius reached for his flies, then felt the father's eyes on him—felt rather than saw, since the man was wearing dark glasses. I am reaching for my privates in the vicinity of his wife and semi-naked child. No, the flies will have to wait. He got back into the car. It was just ten or fifteen minutes to Nîmes, though finding the house could take another quarter of an hour. He was glad he hadn't had a second cup of coffee.

How had he managed to forget about Travis Beggs? A silly question. Actually, anyone might have done so—anyone of his age, that is. His internet searches hadn't turned up much: the Optimex Foundation, brainchild of billionaire Harry D. Selkirk of obscure background, appeared to be a recently instituted all-purpose money-pot with a nebulous ideology attached. The website ('under construction') included a Mission Statement that expressed a generalised beneficence and optimism for the future of humanity together with the conviction that the world's problems could be solved by harnessing the intellectual powers of the best and brightest among us. Such harnessing was evidently to be achieved through financial incentives. A simple concept. The name of Travis Beggs was nowhere to be found on the site, nor on the internet, but that wasn't so surprising. What was surprising was the immediacy with which he'd offered to fly over to France to talk business, rather than waiting for Julius's return. They must want him pretty badly.

He looked forward to telling Philippe about the Optimex Foundation—more doubtful at the thought of telling Maia. Philippe's response would be enjoyably acerbic. For him it would be an opportunity for a lengthy diagnosis, perhaps even a genealogy. Maia was harder to predict. She might worry that Julius was selling his soul; or she might look at him and exclaim 'What a fine project!' He couldn't say. He couldn't say, because she was a more complex person than Philippe, if *complex* was the word, and because he hadn't seen her for so long.

Maia's first words to Julius: 'You look different with your clothes on.' He was sitting having a coffee in Coco's on the Cowley Road. The girl at the next table—petite, frizzy black hair, big brown eyes—addressed him across her hummus and pitta. Julius was quick to get her drift: she was attending the life-drawing classes at the Ruskin at which he regularly appeared naked and draped over some piece of furniture, or standing and staring into the middle distance. By this means he augmented slightly his student grant.

'Doesn't everyone?' he replied.

'I don't know. Seems a fair guess.'

Soon they were talking, and it wasn't long before she suggested she paint his portrait. Apparently he had an 'interesting face'. That meant cycling around to her house in east Oxford every Tuesday and Friday, having some tea and biscuits, and then sitting on a chair in her kitchen for thirty or forty minutes. The chair was planted beneath a circular mirror and he was to sit cross-legged. Fortunately it was quite a big kitchen, and Caleb, Maia's tortoiseshell cat, would generally pay a visit, pacing around the quarry-tiled room in a proprietorial way and sniffing at his legs. They talked of art, politics, Oxford, parents. Maia had endured a miserable childhood going from one set of foster parents to another, only to discover as an adult that her mother had died of a heroin overdose. Julius was amazed by her resilience and good humour. The other thing they talked about of course was God. God was very much Maia's theme; he almost thought of her as having introduced him to it. Her heart's desire was to become a nun. *Disaster!* he said to himself, but then asked himself why he thought that. He never got as far as answering his own question, and with the advent of Johnny the whole issue fell into abeyance.

That portrait was now hanging somewhere in Fournhac with a price tag on it. He wondered what Maia was charging. It was an accomplished piece, he hoped she was asking a decent amount. Somewhere in a cardboard box in England was the painting's photo, given to him by Maia just before he set off for the States, along with a biography of Simone Weil which he subsequently lost on his travels. He felt a certain trepidation at the thought of seeing the painting itself again after all these years. It would be an encounter with his younger, unencumbered self: writer-to-be, husband-to-be, father-to-be.

Mere potentiality—almost a tabula rasa. A tabula rasa wearing a cravat.

It was good talking to Maia on the phone yesterday. Funny how voices change so much less than faces. Hers was smooth and flowing, like a river. Like the river beside which she had been walking, perhaps, the river which once upon a time he used to gaze into from the parapet of the stone bridge. But could she have really seen what she thought she saw there? That was certainly an odd conclusion to their conversation. Maia's world just was an odd world, he reflected, full of noises, sounds and sweet airs. A floating body, a bird rising into the air—such signs and symbols seemed to address themselves to her more than to other people. Her surroundings were shot through with meanings, with hints and clues pointing to something beyond. Maia is a human antenna, he thought. A clairvoyant.

And here was the turnoff for Nîmes.

*

As Philippe had stated, there was a car park a couple of blocks from the house where he was staying, edged by plane trees. Julius slotted between two cars and got out, then found the requisite machine and bought his ticket. Food smells were emerging from a nearby café; he hoped that he and Philippe would go somewhere decent for lunch.

A few minutes later he was standing in front of a green door with buzzers to one side. No names, only numbers. Philippe, or Philippe's friend, occupied flat

19. Julius pressed the button and waited. It was a side street; the noise of traffic was distant and muffled. A radio blared through an open window somewhere behind him.

'Durward!' Second syllable a touch elongated, softened by the ghost of an R. Julius looked around from side to side but could see no one.

'Durward! Above you!'

He peered up. A head and shoulders protruded from a third-storey window, black against the brightness of the sky.

'Philippe!' He waved a hand.

'When you hear a buzz, push the door.'

The head and shoulders disappeared. Julius waited. *Buzz.* He pushed, and found himself in a dim and slightly smelly hallway with a staircase ahead. The door closed behind him. Still dazzled by the sunlight, now quenched, he shuffled with outstretched hand towards where he thought the stairs were. His fingers met with a banister and he stood awhile to allow his vision to get acclimatised. '*Third floor.*' Transmuted by the resonance of the stairwell Philippe's voice floated down to him as something disembodied. Arentz has finally attained the condition of pure spirit, he thought as he climbed the stairs. When he reached the third floor Philippe had gone back into his flat leaving the door open. He wasn't one for effusive welcomes and bear hugs, Julius knew that. The revolutionary has no time for such things. Perhaps they would shake hands. But once Julius was over the threshold he found Philippe's arms around his neck and a scratchy cheek against his own. The gesture touched him disproportionately; maybe he had no idea how much he meant to other people, how often he was in their thoughts or his name was on their lips. Those were the sorts of things about which there was no enquiring (who would one ask?) and so which were left alone. The only, and all-absorbing, exception to this was when you were in love. And yet wasn't friendship just as important?

'Come in,' said Philippe, ushering him into an airy modern apartment more minimalist in its décor than Julius could imagine suited his old friend. No piles of papers and books, no overflowing ashtrays. A flat screen TV dominated the living room, but Philippe was guiding him along to the kitchen dining room 'where we will be more comfortable'. Eventually they stood looking at one another. Philippe had shaved his head and this for some reason enhanced the intensity of his eyes, with their lowering black eyebrows. The broad and full-lipped mouth out of which indictments and prophecies flowed so freely broke into a smile, producing in the cheeks to either side two dimples that seemed to say, 'It's all in play, really. Life isn't *that* serious.' Julius was sure their owner would disagree.

'You're looking well,' he said.

'I'm glad to hear it,' replied Philippe. 'Not that I believe in such things.'

'Ever the ascetic. You'll just have to live it down. Can I use your loo?'

'First on the left through there' (pointing). 'I'll make some coffee.'

When Julius returned Philippe was standing by the kitchen window looking out. The coffee things were on the table. Julius couldn't help asking: 'Have you given up smoking?'

'Yes and no. I have a standing intention to give up one day, but my present abstinence is compelled.'

'Your friend doesn't allow it?'

'Correct. A rule of the establishment.'

'A mere rule, Philippe?'

'*When in Rome* is an adage of self-interest. Not a moral principle.'

'Mightn't it be both?'

'It's possible. But if there's a moral principle involved, it won't have anything to do with the sanctity of rules. I won't fall into your traps, Durward.'

He had sat down and was pouring the coffee. Julius was delighted; they were both playing their parts to perfection. Even Philippe's trembling hand seemed to be putting on a show for the occasion.

'And where is your friend? The non-smoker?'

'Dany has gone to get provisions. He'll be back in half an hour or so. Which gives us enough time to...' He passed Julius a mug.

'Catch up,' finished Julius. 'Chew the fat. Put the world to rights.'

'Exactly. Durward, you read my mind.'

He leant back in his chair and looked up at the ceiling, a characteristic gesture. Julius could almost see the ancient sofa, the packet of Gauloises, stains on the Persian rug. But Philippe's next question was unexpected.

'Have you ever heard of an outfit called CIRI?'

'Seeree? Don't think so.'

'Centre International de Recherche en Infectiologie. Based in Lyon. The people there isolate—or create—dangerous biological agents. With a view, you understand, to fighting infectious diseases around the globe. To understand is to conquer.'

'Ah yes. I know the sort of thing you mean.'

'You have a place in England that's involved in the same business called Porton Down.'

'The guys who developed an anthrax weapon in the 40s.'

'That's right, and tried it out on a small Scottish island which consequently became uninhabitable by mammals for the next sixty years. Well, CIRI, you see, is—officially—completely different from Porton Down since it has nothing to do with the military. As I say, it's simply devoted to the health and welfare of mankind. It also happens to have close connections with the Institute of Virology in Wuhan province from which it seems likely that the Covid-19 virus spread. You remember the 2020 pandemic?'

'Of course I do. I thought it began in a Chinese market.'

The dimples returned. 'A Chinese wet market, yes, that was the going theory, wasn't it. Bats, pangolins, salamanders, civet cats—the real enemies of the human race. But you know as well as I do who the enemies of the human race are.'

'The human race,' Julius obligingly answered. 'But where are you going with all this, Philippe?'

'I will tell you where. Approximately fifteen kilometres north-east of where you are sitting, amid the oak trees and eucalyptuses.'

Julius knew those forests. He had even camped in them as a young man. All that area had belonged to the dukes of Uzès, who would hunt for boar there.

'An offshoot of CIRI, a high-security biolaboratory, is to be built on a site occupying a couple of thousand hectares. With electric fences and watchtowers. Rather like a concentration camp in appearance. Plenty of underground facilities. You see,' Philippe smiled, 'it's important to keep up with the Chinese.'

Julius felt vaguely sick. 'But this is horrible...'

'I'm glad you think so,' said Philippe. 'I thought you would. There are others who feel the same way. This country hasn't yet fallen into a complete political torpor. Julius...' He leant forward, his eyes shining. (With indignation? Excitement?) 'We have to stop them.'

'We?'

'Yes, we. Of course I mean everyone, but I especially mean—we.'

'You and me?'

Philippe nodded. *What is needed is action*: the old refrain. But when had Philippe ever acted on it? He was professionally incapable of turning verbal ploughshares into practical swords.

'What do you have in mind?'

Philippe leaned back again. 'You're a famous writer, Durward. No,' he held up a hand against Julius's protest, 'that book is—deservedly—a landmark. Translated into . . . how many languages? Ten?'

'I don't remember.'

'A portrait of the modern era. A blueprint for Western society. If the author of *Pandora's Mirror* were to put his name to a newspaper article—or it needn't be a newspaper article, a pamphlet, a blog, whatever, exposing the ecological cost, the human folly . . .'

'Put my name to? Do you mean write?'

'Yes, yes, write. And if you want I could help you. What's necessary is for the message to be broadcast to the English-speaking world. It can no longer remain a purely French affair. An outsider's voice will carry further.'

A collaboration—a comradely collaboration. The idea was attractive, Julius warmed to it immediately. But whether it would do any good . . .

'People need to know,' Philippe went on. 'Developing and investigating deadly viruses, viruses which could kill off millions of people and against which there might be no vaccine: *that* is meant to be a grand humanitarian project. Occasionally the mask slips and you hear the whispered admission that, okay, we might after all be thinking about possible military uses—ever so hypothetically, you understand. "They might do it to us first, so we have to be prepared: how else than by creating the stuff they might use on us?" And perhaps we'll want to use it on them first. Can't rule that out; might have to. That's politics.' By now he was pacing round the kitchen, twitching his shoulders and rubbing his shaven head. 'Accidents? Did you say accidents? They don't happen— only to the bad guys. Chernobyl was a *Soviet* disaster. Fukushima? That was a tsunami, they never happen in Languedoc, what are you talking about. Destruction of the forest? Oh, I suppose you'll be protesting against roads next!'

'Philippe, Philippe,' interrupted Julius, 'the answer is yes. Please sit down, you're making me dizzy.'

Philippe stopped his pacing and held out a hand. The handshake is for sealing a deal, thought Julius. They shook hands. Philippe sat down.

'Very good. I thought I could count on you. In fact I knew I could. Julius, I want you to meet some of the people who are going to appear in your report: activists, protesters, excellent boys and girls. A few of them are going to be joining us.'

'Here?'

'Yes, Dany will be bringing them. You know they're very keen to meet you.' Again the disarming dimples. 'And they've already reconnoitred the site. At present there are just a few preliminary sheds and the odd notice stuck to a tree—no bulldozers or *Entreé Interdite* signs yet, but those will be arriving any moment, if they haven't already, along with the floodlights and the sniffer dogs. It's important to act soon.'

Julius recalled that first email: *If you're ever in France, get in touch. I'd like you to meet some friends of mine.* Had

Philippe been 'counting on' him for all this time? Maybe he was more useful than lovable: a publicity agent for the Movement, a famous name on a pamphlet. There were worse fates but it was a trifle—how shall one say—deflating.

'Does your movement have a name?'

'My *movement*?' Philippe laughed. 'There are various groups … Some are more ambitious than others, some are merely local—some are connected, some act alone … If you read the newspapers you might have heard of Rebex, but that's just an umbrella term.'

'Rebex?'

'Yes—inspired by you British, actually. Remember Extinction Rebellion? They caused a certain amount of disruption in London, marching and cycling, that kind of thing. Reb-Ex: Rebellion Extinction, or Rebellion contre l'extinction, I suppose. Naturally the French version aims to be more disruptive than the British one ever was.'

'France has a tradition of revolution.'

'And we are a very traditional people, as you pointed out in your book. Didn't you go so far as to predict that the next ideological upheaval would take place on French soil?'

'Did I?'

'That was how you were interpreted in France.'

'I never checked the translation.'

'Your prediction may yet come true. I hope it does.'

The sound of approaching laughter could be heard. A door opened and it grew louder; there were footsteps and voices, a rustling of paper, and three people appeared, two boys and a girl, all in their twenties, carrying shopping bags. Julius rose from his chair. The chattering stopped. One of the boys, fair haired with a wispy beard and wearing glasses, put his load down and stepped forward. Julius thought he might be about to make a speech. From his seat Philippe intoned, 'Julius, behold the future.'

'Professor Durward?' said the boy. The lenses of his glasses magnified his blue eyes into a look of congealed wonder.

'Oui, c'est moi. Et vous êtes Dany?'

'Oui, je suis…'

'Speak to them in English, Julius. You're the renowned man of letters, remember. And you'll be writing it all up in English.'

Julius smiled benignly. 'Very pleased to meet you, Dany. Thank you for your hospitality.'

Dany blushed. 'It's an honour, Professor Durward.' He glanced over at Philippe and huskily corrected himself: 'Julius.'

'And this is Eva and this is Laurent,' said Philippe. Julius extended his smile to the remaining pair, an athletic-looking girl and a boy in an unseasonal duffle coat. Eva grinned back while Laurent nodded over a large paper bag clasped to his chest. Julius found it hard to imagine him scaling an electric fence.

The shopping bags contained the ingredients for lunch, it turned out. Julius and Philippe retreated to the living room while the youngsters prepared the meal.

'It's a little early but I know you have to go on to somewhere else afterwards,' said Philippe.

'A place called Fournhac. Do you know it? My old friend Maia lives there.'

Philippe raised his thick eyebrows politely but incuriously. His mind is on higher things, thought Julius, such as the destruction of the planet.

Over salads, bread, hard-boiled eggs and wine he learnt more about the feelings and aspirations of Philippe's protégés. They had all been his students in Paris but at different times, Dany being the oldest, Eva the youngest. Dany now worked as an IT consultant in Nîmes, Eva as a gardener for the bourgeoisie and Laurent was unemployed. Eva and Laurent lived respectively in Paris and Nantes, from which Julius deduced that, like Philippe, they had descended on Dany for the sole purpose of meeting and talking with the author of *Pandora's Mirror*. Not the sole purpose however: they must also have been laying plans for the occupation/ sabotage of the projected virology institute.

'What are you planning to do?' he asked cutting into a tomato. 'Do you really think you can stop them?'

Laurent said, 'Why not? If there are enough protests all over France, the government, it will fear the unpopularity, it will fear to not be elected again. And there are many protests, not just about CIRI, about other things— the climate, the pollution. Many protests.' Defiantly he broke off a piece of baguette.

'But what are you going to do on the site itself? Chain yourselves to the trees?'

'Some of us will be in the trees, yes,' said Eva. 'There will probably be many arrests. It will . . . il obstruera . . .'

'Clog up.'

'Yes. It will clog up the law courts and the police vans. Like with Gandhi's protests.'

'Some of our actions can be performed remotely—at a distance.' It was Dany: he spoke softly, precisely.

'Dany knows a lot about computers,' explained Philippe, leaning over for the wine bottle. Eva, sitting next to him, took charge of it to spare his trembling fingers the task of pouring. As she filled his glass he laid a grateful hand on her shoulder.

'Do you mean you can hack into their systems?' asked Julius.

Dany gave a coy shrug and mumbled something.

'Much easier than you think,' commented Laurent.

Eva's hand had joined Philippe's; the fingers intertwined.

'If you hack into their systems and they catch you, they can put you away for a very long time. And if the Americans are involved in any way . . .'

'Unlikely,' murmured Philippe.

' . . . then that means a few decades in solitary confinement.' He reached for an egg. A telephone.

'It's possible to cover all one's traces,' said Dany. 'Completely.'

Eva was whispering something into Philippe's ear. The egg was ringing.

'Some of the other group members, they are happy to damage—to do some damage,' said Laurent. He grinned: 'Max recommends the Dark Web.'

Intertwining. The doctor spoke, but Julius couldn't catch what he was saying. Something about... 'Speak up, the line's bad.'

Philippe was looking at him. Eva seemed to be crying. A sudden deterioration apparently, the boy had already lost consciousness, better come quickly.

'Durward, are you okay?'

It's not your fault, it's not our fault, Toni please don't cry, I love you Toni. The telephone had stopped singing or ringing. Eva was on her feet now, not crying after all. Julius reached for her fingers, Toni's fingers.

'Get him some water.'

For some reason they were all moving about, talking in funny concerned voices. Somebody put a glass of water in front of him. Philippe was standing over him saying words. Words, words, words. Intertwined.

'Intertwined.'

'What?'

'Intertwined. Everything is intertwined.'

'Julius, you're not making any sense.'

'Everything is intertwined with everything.' He gestured at Eva. 'Like her.'

Eva pointed at herself and her lips formed a silent *Moi?* Julius crumpled up. His shoulders shook and he bent his head. Laurent put an arm around him. Philippe produced some brandy and gradually he steadied, came back to earth. They had all moved into the living room and he was sitting on a sofa. The window was open. Fresh air and the blare of a radio at street level entered into the room, confirmers of an independent reality. He tried to make light of his episode; all those concerned eyes on him were too burdensome. They probably wanted to ask him questions. Well, they could ask Philippe, Philippe would fill them in all right. Once he had gone. Philippe knew… of course he didn't know about the Alethex and all that, but he knew about Julius's marriage, he knew about Toni and how they'd met in the States when Julius, and how their child had got ill, little… little Cécile—very ill. No. Not Cécile. It was a boy. A boy called

'You should come and see the site,' said Philippe. 'It's a beautiful place, dense forest, ancient trees.'

A boy called

'And you can meet some of the others.'

'Like Max,' said Laurent.

'Like Max.'

A boy called

'I'll arrange it. In a day or two.'

A boy

IV

TRAVIS POCKETED HIS PHONE. 'SORTED. Friday at 2 p.m.'

Kelly said, 'So you've spoken to the great man. How does that feel?'

He shrugged. 'You can't tell much from someone's voice. He seemed kind of confused, like he'd forgotten all about me.'

Kelly leaned into him, her nose burrowing in his collar. 'Poor little Trav, forgotten about by the Great Man.'

'What's that perfume you've got on?' complained Travis, wriggling away. He stressed the *fume* of 'perfume'. Kelly sat back in her seat and looked out of the window at the terminal building. It was certainly cuter than Luton airport.

The crocodile of passengers began shifting at last towards the front of the plane, British holidaymakers mainly, couples, the odd kid ... a few French people, the women chic and the men looking self-satisfied. Kelly wondered what it would be like going to bed with one. You'd need mirrors, wouldn't you, the guy could probably only get it up if he had a mirror to admire himself in.

'Trav, do you think I'm a racist?'

Travis was struggling out of his seat. 'You're Australian, how can you be a racist?'

'Sweet,' murmured Kelly, looking back out of the window.

When they'd gone through passport control and were waiting for their luggage by the carousel Travis became aware of the number of armed police in the building. They stood in groups of two or three, torsos bulging with bullet-proof vests, guns pointing heavenwards. Kelly had obviously noticed the same thing; she flashed a smile at a nearby cop on whose thick neck a tattoo sat like an intricate plague spot.

'Why all the security?' she said, turning to Travis. 'D'you think it's a drugs bust?'

'I've no idea.' He'd seen his suitcase. The conveyor belt delivered it up to him and he swung it away from the company of its newfound friends onto the floor at his feet. The carousel trundled on. Finally Kelly's suitcase and backpack emerged, a couple of stragglers, out of the black hole. Travis did the honours and the two of them made for the exit.

Twenty minutes later they were walking towards the Hertz section of the car rental park, foreshortened shadows moving before them on the warm asphalt. 'Let's find a place to eat,' said Travis. He had queued patiently to get the car keys and fill in all the paperwork. Some refreshment was needed, preferably at a café table on a

Nîmes pavement. Since his interview with the professor had been postponed by forty-eight hours he could take it easy. Would Durward take the bait? That was the question. The fee was a fat one, but apparently not so enticing as to stop the professor wandering off somewhere absent-mindedly. Part of Travis was piqued at being stood up. Academics were as ditsy as hell, of course, you had to factor that in. Hopefully the sight of Kelly would focus his mind a little ... I'm being flippant, he thought, maybe he really was called away on important business. In any case, I'm not an independent actor, what I do I do on behalf of the Optimex Foundation, with the ultimate goal of bettering the lot of humanity - plus the subsidiary goal of impressing Uncle Harry. I'm on an assignment, as you might say.

In Nîmes he found a small car park overlooked by plane trees and parked his Citroën next to a white Peugeot. Getting out of the car he smelt onions frying and thought of beer.

'My thighs were sticking to the leather in there,' said Kelly banging her door shut. 'The police could take my prints off the seat. Did you ever photocopy your bum, Trav?'

It wasn't long before the beer materialised, along with a glass of rosé for Kelly. Two pizzas were on their way. They sat at a table under an awning, early diners with a view of traffic, pigeons and, across the car park, a church. The temperature was perfect. It was Kelly's first trip to France and her second holiday with Travis. She had met him six months previously: a nice enough guy and apparently blood relative to some serious American money. He'd taken her across the pond to meet his billionaire uncle at the beginning of the summer and her antipodean charm had softened the old man up to the point where he could say, scrawny hand upon her knee, 'I like you, kid.'

Now Travis was looking at her. What did that expression mean? She knew it wasn't adoration. Adoration could be a pain in the neck, she was glad it wasn't that. Ownership? It wasn't quite ownership—nor was it mere sexual appreciation, though that obviously came into it. Curiosity? She was an exotic specimen after all, something like a koala or a duck-billed platypus, one that could crack jokes and give blowjobs. She smiled back at him.

'Those earrings are nice,' he said.

She took one off, a chunky wooden triangle of many hues, and handed it to him. 'Don't pull the pin,' she said matter-of-factly.

'Why would I?'

'No reason, but if you did you might spill coke on the table. That's all.'

He stared at her. 'Are you kidding?'

Kelly shook her head and took a sip of rosé.

'Are you *crazy*? If they'd caught you with this stuff we'd be ...' He put the earring down on the table as if it might burn his fingers.

'Not *we*, Trav; I wouldn't drag you into jail if you didn't want to come. But it's totally safe.' She returned the wooden triangle to her ear. 'I've done it hundreds of times.'

'You ... are you ... that's ...'

'Trav, you're being incoherent.'

'What about sniffer dogs?'

'Why d'you think I put this perfume on? Foxes them completely.'

His mouth was hanging open. A waiter arrived, and as the pizzas and cutlery were set before them Travis's open mouth began to emit laughter, a crescendo of raucous captivated laughter that caused the heads of passers-by to turn. Eventually he said, 'Both earrings? Or just the one?'

'Both, of course. Otherwise I'd feel lopsided.' Kelly tilted her head, squinted, and stuck her tongue goofily out of one side of her lipsticked mouth.

'Not just a dumb blonde,' Travis concluded. 'Right?'

'Right.' She picked up a pizza segment. 'If you're good you can have some.'

Under the table their feet met.

*

After lunch they walked into town to see what there was to see and came across a Coliseum lookalike in front of which ('But where *is* the front, Trav?') a bronze matador draped his bronze cloak upon the ground. Kelly got herself photographed beside him or it, craning her pouting face up towards his, one foot flung out behind her. Tourists milled around, scooters and motorbikes darted among them and the paving stones threw back the warmth of the sun. This was definitely feeling like a holiday—a proper European holiday, too, with churches and cobbled streets and strange road signs. No beachwear anywhere.

'It's also an assignment,' said Travis. 'I have to persuade the dude, Kelly. Got to keep my wits about me.'

They were strolling down a side street full of people and shops.

'Don't you worry, we'll persuade him,' she said. 'It just takes charm and we both have bucketloads.'

'I think he might be more serious than that. His book's pretty serious. All about the state of the world, the mess we're in, that kind of stuff. Plus he lost a kid.'

'Lost a kid?' She frowned. 'That's shit. How do you know?'

'My uncle told me. He must have got it from some profile or interview in the papers. He knows a lot about Julius Durward, he's done a lot of research.'

They walked on in silence for a bit.

'This book,' said Kelly, 'is it any good? I mean, do you think it's, like, important?'

'Uncle Harry thinks it's the most important document since Karl Marx's *Das Kapital*. I haven't read *Das Kapital* so I wouldn't know. There's a lot of history, a lot of politics, some anthropology, psychology ... He's woven in some interviews with other academics and people. It's doing a lot of things.'

'Is there a message?'

'Well—maybe messages, plural. Or parables or something. He talks about the history of revolutions, how different kinds of discontent produce different kinds of revolution; how the identity of the hate object determines the nature of the hatred and how it gets manifested...'

'What's a hate object?'

'It's what you hate. You might hate a particular king or dynasty—or a particular religion—or foreigners in your midst—or the police—or the fact that they've changed the calendar without asking. Whatever. A lot of hatred gets expressed in physical violence but that's not the only form of expression; it might play out in words or rituals or works of art. Or it might implode, or turn into something completely different.'

'Sounds like you know this book off by heart.'

'I've read it a couple of times. Remember I have an assignment.'

'Softly softly catchee monkey. You said he talks about the mess we're in. What sort of mess? Does he think we're going to have a revolution?'

'Unclear. Unclear to me at any rate. But he does think we're full of hatred. So...'

'Hatred of what?'

'Hatred of ourselves. I think.'

'Seems to me there's a lot of self-love around.'

'He'd probably say that was the same thing.'

'A book of riddles, then.'

Ahead of them, sitting on a camp stool in front of a shop window in which scantily-clad mannequins struck poses, a busker strummed a guitar and sang into a microphone, ignored by the stream of shoppers and tourists.

He sat by himself, wrapped up in his own performance. It wasn't even clear if he wanted money; there was no bucket or open guitar case inviting contributions. Kelly stopped to listen. It was an old song from a vanished world: *Yesterday* by the Beatles, a young man's plaint sublimed into something more universal. The song was its own elegy. Kelly felt its wistfulness in her stomach—she read it in the singer's face as he sang with eyes closed, head swaying, *Why she had to go, I don't know, she wouldn't say.* She just passed away, things do pass away, they don't tell us why they're going. Time passes, today becomes yesterday, mystified we shake our heads. Eventually the song itself comes to an end.

Travis put a hand on her arm. 'Kelly?'

She turned to face him and he saw that her eyes were moist.

'You're a funny girl,' he smiled. 'It's time we went to Uzès. I'll buy you an ice cream first.'

The road from Nîmes to Uzès is the D979 and to either side of it lies beautiful countryside. Travis drove with the windows down since he disliked air conditioning. Kelly would probably have preferred an open top if she'd had the option. In Virginia he'd driven her around in one of his uncle's old sports cars, half way up the Blue Ridge Parkway and back again, staying a couple of nights at a bed and breakfast. Uncle Harry had suggested the idea; maybe he was living vicariously, a widower with a vivid imagination. Or he just liked them both and wanted them to have a good time. It was on that holiday that Uncle Harry put a copy of *Pandora's Mirror* into Travis's hand and said: 'I want you to read this book and tell me what you think of it. I have a proposal to make to you.' Kelly was somewhere else—in the swimming pool, most likely—and Travis had the impression he was involved in some sort of man-to-man interaction. The word 'proposal' naturally triggered thoughts of remunerative employment, and since he had recently lost his job at the BBC he was more than happy to go off with this bestseller from the previous decade and curl up in a corner of Uncle Harry's southern mansion with a view to extracting its wisdom. It turned out to be a more rewarding read than he'd anticipated. Over the next ten days or so Uncle Harry would pester him with 'How's the book going, Travis?' to which he was able to reply truthfully, 'It's going well, sir', until finally he approached his uncle, ensconced in a hammock, with the news that he'd finished it. He must have acquitted himself well in the ensuing interrogation or interview because before the hour was out Uncle Harry had explained to him the aims and ideals of the newly conceived Optimex Foundation and appointed him PA to the Director (viz Uncle Harry) on a very respectable starting salary.

'Julius Durward is, to my mind, a genius,' his uncle told him as they strolled around the gardens of the estate. 'What I get from his book is a clear message, a message of hope. Think of it: never in the entire history of the human race has there been as much knowledge as there is today, painstakingly amassed over the centuries—science, technology, economics, psychology—and all this amassing of knowledge is, it must be, leading up to a revolution, Travis, a glorious revolution. It's that revolution which Durward seems to me to be continually hinting at. We human beings have the capacity...' The old man stood still, a thin stooping figure holding up a bony and didactic index finger—'...to eliminate all suffering; to put an end to disease and deformity, poverty and destitution. To put an end, in fact...' He lowered his voice and his wrinkled face came up close to his nephew's—'...to death itself.'

Uncle Harry was into cryogenics. His interest in the subject was both personal and financial, speculative in both senses. Having made his fortune in construction and pharmaceuticals, and having salved his conscience by means of a few donations to universities and to the more outré species of charity, Uncle Harry looked at his remaining billions and asked himself the question, 'What do I want just for myself?' The answer came readily enough: 'Immortality.' But this wasn't mere selfishness or fear of death; he was in addition genuinely attracted to the picture of a post-mortal world, banks upon banks of deep-frozen tissue getting reanimated by future scientists and leaping out of warmed-up caskets to dance the dance of the risen dead. This was surely going to happen, it was surely our shared destiny. The grain of truth in all the world religions would finally bring forth fruit in the soil of modern science. 'Death, where is thy sting?' asked St Paul and John Donne responded with 'Death, thou shalt die.' Harry D. Selkirk concurred.

Where there is manifest destiny there is opportunity for investment. An institution in Texas had received a certain sum to be spent on the design and development of new methods of vitrification and similar projects in China and Abu Dhabi were being funded. It was hoped that a return on these investments would start to materialise once initial successes began to be rewarded by increased demand from would-be beneficiaries. ('Rich old bastards, you mean,' Kelly remarked when Travis explained it all to her.) What any of this had to do with *Pandora's Mirror* Travis found it hard to say, but he could see why his uncle wanted to have Julius Durward give the inaugural lecture: he was a high-profile, or fairly high-profile, intellectual who had written a book about the state of things. Most of the people in the audience presumably wouldn't have read the book but they would probably have heard of it and of its author.

'Where's the lecture to be given, sir? In the UK? Or over here?'

The two men were sitting in a wooden gazebo which looked down over an artificial lake. A grey squirrel eyed them expressionlessly from its position a couple of yards off.

'That's for him to choose,' said Uncle Harry. 'If he wants to give it in London, I can hire a suitable venue. That Wembley place perhaps. Or he might want to do it in his own university, on his own turf. On the other hand we could have it in New York, with a reception at the Plaza or somewhere. Let him decide, the important thing is that you persuade him to do it. I won't be there myself.'

'Won't be at the lecture? But you're the . . .'

'No, Travis. I don't want to see him and he probably won't want to see me. What matters isn't whether our carcasses come into contact, what matters is that our *ideas* come together in public, that the guiding spirit of *Pandora's Mirror* lends itself to the inception of this project. The Optimex Foundation is going to be like nothing else on the planet. I mean to change the world, Travis.'

He was gazing into the distance. A skittish breeze played with his thinning hair and a fly had settled on his shirt collar.

'And after the inaugural lecture—do you have anyone else lined up, sir? Any other events planned?'

'Sure. In outline. But settling on the details is going to be your job. If you can get together a shortlist of names and CVs, I'll happily take that for my starting point. We can talk some more about this over dinner,' he concluded, getting to his feet. 'If your girl doesn't mind.'

*

Uncle Harry's mansion was called The Vines. It dated from the first decade of the nineteenth century and as its name suggested had once boasted a considerable vineyard. This, however, Uncle Harry had uprooted, being himself a teetotaller and regarding wine as a poor business proposition. On the grave of the vineyard he had erected a gym and an observatory. Kelly and Travis got the guided tour on the evening of their arrival and were invited to view the night sky through what their host referred to as the most powerful privately owned telescope in Virginia. Travis asked a series of polite questions about the specifications of the instrument. He still bore towards his uncle some of the uneasy apprehensiveness of childhood, but over the next few days the feeling subsided as he digested the fact that the irascible and sarcastic inhabitant of his memory had been replaced by a mellower and above all smaller human being.

'You're looking at Saturn,' said Uncle Harry to Kelly. 'See the rings?'

'Loud and clear,' she replied. She was standing with one hand resting on the great tube of the telescope, her face up to the eyepiece, long blonde hair falling down her back, feet planted slightly apart. Uncle Harry's eyes slid up two lovely legs to a pair of tight denim shorts and Travis saw a look of something like pain pass across his face. The old man had been happily married for forty years when his wife Doreen died suddenly of a stroke during a holiday on the Riviera. (He had never been back to Europe.) That was about ten years ago, but it was only within the last couple of years that Travis had begun receiving communications from his mother's half-brother. As for his mother herself, she was languishing in a care home in Bristol, a victim of Parkinson's disease.

The union of Harry and Doreen had been a childless one. Travis wondered idly what had become of Doreen—whether she was lying in a freezer somewhere or had gone up in smoke. Ice or fire. He felt instinctively that his uncle must have opted for one of those alternatives: gradual decomposition underground would have presented too indefinite a picture, neither one thing nor the other. Uncle Harry was an all or nothing man. I'm being flippant again, he thought, he probably misses her like hell. This sudden gust of high-voltage femininity I've brought into his life will be confusing for him, liable to put him off balance.

'It's amazing, Mr Selkirk,' Kelly said, directing her perfect smile at him. 'Such incredible detail. Do you think there's life out there?'

'Intelligent life, d'you mean?'

'Yes.'

A look of surprised interest came into Uncle Harry's face. Here was a girl who knew the significance of the night sky. Maybe like him she could see in the panoply of stars the presence of a beckoning finger: 'Come, explore, discover.'

'I certainly do think so. Mathematically it's a near certainty, given the number of planets and the age of the universe.'

'Plus the properties of carbon, hydrogen et cetera,' added Kelly.

Both men stared at her. Uncle Harry was struggling to reconcile this remark with the denim shorts and blonde hair. Travis had simply never heard her sound erudite before. ('We don't talk chemistry, that's why, Trav,' she explained later. 'Do you want to?')

'Well...' mumbled Uncle Harry, and his head twisted on his thin neck in a kind of pleasant discomfiture. 'What say we have a little refreshment? You two must be famished.'

Supper that evening was eaten in an oak-panelled but cosy room on the first floor, prepared and served up by the estate factotum, a Mexican called Nico. For most of the remaining holiday they ate together on the veranda, the main exception being the two evenings Kelly and Travis spent away up at that B & B in the Blue Ridge Mountains. But on their last night Uncle Harry once again invited them up to the oak-panelled room where Nico pulled out all the stops, presenting a stew suffused with the flavour of smoked chipotle peppers. In honour of the two guests beer was provided. The room was illuminated by candles.

'Nico, this is delicious,' enthused Travis.

'Where would I be without him,' said Uncle Harry. 'He's my life support system, aren't you Nico? Finest cook, gardener and handyman in the state of Virginia. When Doreen died I was all at sea, didn't know what to do with myself, almost couldn't look after myself, and then Nico appears like an angel sent down from heaven.' He slurped some stew. 'Not that I'm a religious man, as you know.'

'Is that her?' asked Kelly, pointing to an oil painting above the unused fireplace—a hyperrealistic depiction of a stocky woman in a yellow dress standing next to a rosebush.

'Yes, that is Doreen's portrait. And in the urn on the mantelpiece are her ashes.'

Fire not ice, thought Travis.

*

Kelly had half unpacked. On the double bed were scattered clothes, bags, a laptop and an epilator. She had interrupted the procedure to check her phone for messages and had got distracted by newsfeeds. Travis sat in a chair in the corner of the hotel room with a bottle of beer out of the fridge. Two French windows opened onto a balcony from which you looked out over the red rooftops of Uzès towards the cathedral.

'All those police at the airport were on account of ecoterrorists, apparently,' said Kelly.

'Uh-huh.'

'Something called Rebex.'

'Uh-huh.'

'Sounds like an indigestion remedy. *Heartburn? Gas? Farting too much? Get NEW Rebex, comes in three different flavours.*'

Travis snorted.

'Seriously though, what do they think's going to happen? Someone puts a bomb on a plane?'

'They might fly drones over the airport,' said Travis. 'It's happened before.'

'And one of those armed cops shoots it down with his Kalashnikov? Pretty heavy-handed if you ask me.'

'Maybe the police presence is meant to reassure people. So they don't get scared about flying. Could be counterproductive, of course.' He took a drink of beer. 'Shall we have some of that coke?'

'In a minute. Trav, does your uncle believe in climate change?'

'Why shouldn't he?'

'He's so into the wonders of technology he might not like the idea of it finally biting us all in the bum. Everything's meant to get better and better, isn't it.'

'Technology can self-correct. If the earth's getting too hot, put solar panels all over the Gobi Desert—that's how Uncle Harry would approach the matter. I guess he's a sort of Darwinist about technology. Bad technology will die out, leaving all the good stuff free to roam the planet.'

'Right, and although the dinosaurs obeyed the Theory of Evolution as best they could they just turned out to be bad technology. It's always too late by the time you discover you're unfit to survive.'

She was rummaging in a bag. Out of it came a circular mirror, which she set down on the coffee table. Then she unhooked an earring and knelt down beside the table.

'I gotta see this,' said Travis getting out of his chair. Onto the surface of the mirror a white powder was being sprinkled, emerging from one corner of the wooden triangle like water from a tap.

'Designed and created by my brother,' said Kelly. 'We're a talented family.'

'Patent pending, right?'

A five euro note had appeared out of the same bag, which Kelly rolled into a tube. She handed the tube to Travis and started shifting and cutting the cocaine with a razor blade. Soon two neat lines lay side by side, chaste lovers touching only their own reflections, not long for this world. Kelly passed the mirror to Travis. 'All yours, Tarzan.' Travis leant over the mirror.

They were on the bed. Kelly's things were now scattered all around the room. Travis, who still wore his socks, looked up at Kelly with her head thrown back, rocking backwards and forwards, the evening sun which streamed through the French windows turning her hair into a luminous confusion. 'You're beautiful,' he managed to say, and she squeezed his left hand in response while his right hand found and cupped her breast and the lava surged through his veins. He closed his eyes and saw a bronze matador, red cape frozen in mid air. Rockaby ba-a-a-aby...

*

The airport taxi, wobbling and shimmering in the heat thrown up by the asphalt, shrank and finally disappeared as it turned a corner of the driveway. Uncle Harry had stopped waving a while ago. He was standing with Nico on the front porch of The Vines.

'A nice pair of kids, don't you think, Nico?'

'Yes sir, very nice.'

'My nephew's grown up to be a sensible young man. His head's screwed on tight enough. No drifting around the world frittering away the days and weeks.'

'No sir.'

'And the girl's bright. Make a good wife for him. Pretty, too.'

'Very pretty, sir.'

'Prettier than Doreen was.' He cleared his throat. 'But Doreen had a beautiful soul, a beautiful soul.'

'Yes sir.'

Selkirk turned to go back into the house. Nico disappeared discreetly. It was a few hours till lunch; after some consideration Selkirk decided to go to the library where he could look over some books and articles, maybe do some planning for Optimex, maybe doze a little in his favourite armchair. 'A house needs a library,' he had told his newly wedded wife half a century ago; 'this place already has one.' And it had: a long well-lit room with bookshelves all along one side from floor to ceiling. The previous inhabitant of The Vines hadn't used it much—a few paperbacks and an untouched encyclopaedia (12 vols) were the library's sole literary contents when the Selkirks moved in—but Mr Selkirk, as in other matters, had great plans for this room as well as for his own intellectual development. He was soon filling up those shelves, partly under his own steam and partly guided by the friendly advice of better-educated acquaintances. A nineteenth century oak step ladder was introduced and a Persian runner laid down on the wooden floor. The room was beginning to look like a library. The process of filling the bookshelves accelerated once Selkirk had taken out subscriptions to a number of periodicals, but after two years he had still only managed to fill half the space. 'Why not put in some ornaments, Harry?' suggested Doreen. 'China figurines are nice. Or you could have little bowls of pot pourri.' Her husband grimaced at the thought. But in time he was visited by a happy inspiration: he would become a collector of fossils. An air of learning could only be enhanced by the presence of fossils, arranged in twos and threes at intervals along the shelves, possibly accompanied by explanatory cards. Once this feat was accomplished (he had decided against the cards) there was still quite a lot of empty space left, but Selkirk felt he'd broken the back of the problem and was able to turn his mind to other things, like the observatory.

He picked up a copy of *New Scientist* and began to read the list of contents. The latest issues of journals and magazines were deposited by Nico on an oval table in an ever-evolving display from which Selkirk could cherry-pick whenever he wandered into the library. 'What Anti-matter tells us about the Origins of the Universe.' He looked at another magazine. 'Are you a Sociopath? Signs and Symptoms.' No. He wasn't in the mood for such things. He turned away and walked over to an armchair with a small table by its side and a halogen reading lamp peering over its shoulder. On the table was his copy of *Pandora's Mirror*, signed by the author, purchased on the internet. A 'used' copy. He had given Travis his spare. 'Take it with you, you'll need to read it a few more times before the message really hits home.' 'Yes sir, thank you sir.'

Selkirk eased himself into the chair and placed a liver-spotted hand over the book as though protecting it. He didn't need to read it any more, its thoughts had been transferred to him, absorbed, sometimes translated ... On paper Julius Durward was a historian and he, Selkirk, was a businessman with a science background, yet they were fellow spirits, they could both perceive the tendencies of things, both read the future in the past. All the great thinkers were predictors, Marx, Darwin, Nietzsche, and in a way they all predicted the same thing—perfection. The kingdom of heaven on earth, if you will. Even if they didn't always know that's what they were doing. The history of humanity was the history of continual improvement. There must be struggle, yes, but it was a struggling free: free of the bonds that hold us back, of the mud on our boots that weighs us down. We cast off the diseased and unworkable, if necessary we kill the runt of the litter. Our destiny calls us. What was the role of the Optimex Foundation in all of this? It was the role of midwife.

And Julius Durward would instigate this great project by bringing the Foundation before the public eye. His inaugural lecture would in effect be the opening sentence of Selkirk's manifesto for the world, which itself would be an agent for global change potentially affecting the lives of millions of human beings. He had just sent his nephew back to London with the brief of persuading Durward to do this thing. Travis was a personable young man. £10,000 was a lot of money.

And that girl is sexy as hell, he thought, then frowned. How was that relevant? It wasn't. He shifted in his seat. Julius Durward would see the imperative of this opportunity, he was bound to.

A grandfather clock standing in a corner of the library struck eleven.

Doreen hadn't much liked the library. She preferred to spend time in the extensive gardens, tending the flowers, having new things planted. 'My wife has a special relationship with the vegetable kingdom,' he used to say to people and in his voice pride and amusement were mingled. 'Harry's never happier than when he's turning the pages of some old book,' was her counter. 'Or handling an old fossil.' And people would laugh indulgently; Harry and Doreen were just made for each other, weren't they—similar yet different, able to poke fun at one another. Never arguing or at each other's throats. Shame they never had any children.

Not strictly true: Doreen had suffered a miscarriage in the second year of their marriage, after which the doctors advised that it would be dangerous to try again. For a time she had fallen into a depression, but SSRIs helped her out of that. His knowledge of the pharmaceutical world had given him the confidence to suggest this course of action in the face of Doreen's half-hearted opposition, and it was only years later, after the stroke, that he began to be troubled—haunted was too strong a word—by misgivings. Irrational, of course, since there was no evidence of any link between SSRIs and strokes. And she had certainly led a happier life than she would have otherwise. We ought to be grateful for the drugs which are on the market these days. Think of all the suffering they've prevented. Human ingenuity has found solutions to the problems of neurochemical misery as straightforward as the action of turning off a tap. You'd be a fool to reject such discoveries—might as well reject the tap in your kitchen.

And his sister? Parkinson's was a harder nut to crack. He was sure they must be working on it, it was probably just a matter of a few years before a cure was developed. Might come too late for Deborah, of course. He hadn't talked with Travis about the boy's mother during his visit, it didn't seem appropriate. Or relevant. Neither of them could do much for Deborah now. Though I guess I am doing something for her, he thought. I'm giving her son a chance in life. It's what I'd do for my own son. If I'd had one.

That was another respect in which he and Durward were similar: each had lost a child. Makes you fix your gaze all the more firmly on the future and on the state of humanity as a whole. A dead child floats away down the river of time, not so much a real thing as a might-have-been-something. A nothing, in fact.

It's nothing, Doreen, don't you see? Nothing at all. Go to sleep now.

Nico, who with noiseless steps had entered the library, observed his employer dozing in his favourite armchair, one hand resting on a book. He watched him in silence. Under the factotum's indifferent gaze the old man's lips parted in a crack out of which emerged a trickle of saliva.

V

THE NOTE WAS WHERE SHE had left it on the kitchen table, a few inches from a wax-dribbled wine bottle. Protruding from the bottle's neck was the stub of a candle, witness to last night's intimate meandering conversation. *Gone for bread and croissants—back soon.* Julius must still be in bed, she thought, resting her shopping bag on the table and crumpling up the note. Probably sleep is what he needs—the oblivion of deep sleep. It's waking oblivion that he's struggling against. There are oblivions and oblivions, just as there are rememberings and rememberings. Strange truth: that something which it's painful to remember can be still more painful to forget.

Maia unloaded the baguettes, the croissants, the pains au chocolat. She hung the shopping bag on a cupboard doorknob, took down three willow pattern plates from the pine dresser which dominated the kitchen (it had looked smaller in the antiques yard where she and Johnny picked it up), and filled the kettle from the tap. As she put the kettle on the hob the ceiling above her head creaked; Julius was awake.

He'd arrived yesterday later than expected. The hire car drew up outside *Les Pêcheurs* at about five o'clock when Maia was listening to the radio news. She had been looking forward to his arrival on and off since waking; now, at the sound of the car door slamming, she hurried out of the pub entrance and almost collided with him. Each exclaimed the other's name and Julius dropped his suitcase onto the path so as to put his arms round her. When he stood back she saw how pale he was, and that his eyes were red, as if he'd been crying. But he was smiling—ah, that smile! Warm, shy, with an air of questioning about it. Their two smiles joined up like grassfire and in a moment they were laughing, it was a conflagration of laughter. But later on he told her that he had been crying.

He told her much that evening. After describing the hotel, his walks around Uzès, how the town was different and yet the same; after asking her about *Les Pêcheurs* and the exhibition; after some 'Do you remember when…?' and 'Are there still…?' and 'Isn't the news awful?'; after all these as you might call them preliminaries he had started to tell her about the illness, beginning with a description of its first manifestations—the odd slip, the odd blip, occurrences sporadic and separated like the first few drops of rain that will eventually become a downpour. There was nothing worthy of notice at that stage, it was a mere source of annoyance, the annoyance gradually evolving into frustration, evolving into panic. Into blind panic, if you weren't careful. 'I don't want to lose my past,' he had said to his doctor, 'it's all I have. It's all any of us has.' His doctor gave him a funny look but referred him to a consultant all the same. The consultant prescribed Alethex.

'Early onset Alzheimer's is something we can't rule out,' the man had said. 'Whether it's that or some other condition, I would expect you to benefit from this medication, really a quite remarkable development—there's a Nobel Prize in there, I shouldn't wonder; I'd certainly take the drug myself if I were in your situation. We'll start you on a low dose then build it up, assuming there are no side-effects.'

'Such as?'

'Such as damage to your liver. Or certain psychological changes: euphoria, confabulation, psychosis... Unlikely to occur. But possible. These things are very dependent on individual biochemistry.'

Seated at the kitchen table, half a bottle of wine between them, Maia asked him: 'And *have* you had any side-effects?'

'I don't know,' he answered. 'I can't tell.'

'What do you mean?'

'Well... my liver's all right, I suppose, but how is one to tell the difference between euphoria and real happiness? Or between paranoia and understandable fear? Or in general between going mad and perceiving the sadness and futility of the world?'

'The world isn't sad and futile, Julius, and you aren't going mad. Some terrible things have happened to you. You lost a son, your marriage collapsed. Those are terrible things. But what if you'd never met Toni or never had a son? Would your life have gone better for that?'

'I forgot his name.'

'What?'

He passed a hand across his brow. 'Earlier today, when I was with Philippe, I . . . my mind had a jolt—from seeing something, seeing a girl's fingers . . . Things started coming back, replaying themselves, Toni, the doctor . . .' He halted.

'And?' She put her hand on top of his.

'Philippe was talking about his usual stuff, politics, protest . . . I was sitting on the sofa, I thought I was feeling better, my mind had clicked back into place seemingly . . . It was embarrassing but it was over, the fit, the episode. And then I tried to think about him and I couldn't remember his name. I'd lost his name.'

'Paul's?' she said softly and he nodded.

'But it came back?'

'Yes. This time.'

And this morning, what? The ceiling creaked some more above her head and the kettle on the hob began to whistle. Maia spooned four scoops of ground coffee into a jug then poured in the hot water and stirred it with the spoon. As she brought the jug over to the table a shaft of sunlight from the window above the kitchen sink fell on the circle-stained tablecloth. The candle-winebottle glinted, awake, and at the same moment Julius appeared in the doorway in his dressing gown.

*

After she saw the shoe in the rushes, the shoe bobbing up and down in the water to the sound of a curlew's flapping wings, Maia said goodbye to Julius and phoned the police. Vincent had been right. A man's body was floating in the river. Peaceful little Fournhac became a crime scene, and within half an hour three police cars and an ambulance had descended on the town, attracting a gaggle of spectators. Young boys eager for the sight of a real corpse ran up and down the river bank shouting excitedly of *meutre*. George took a break from his house decorating job to stroll down and engage the police in conversation. Vincent, vindicated, stood centre stage with his arms folded. But Maia stayed away: she would hear about it all soon enough and in any case had to go up to the barn to be ready for the opening of the exhibition.

If anything, the body in the river helped the opening night go with a bang. People wanted to talk about it, to share details and exchange theories, and that meant meeting in a public place. *Les Pêcheurs* was the obvious venue and a number of citizens began their evening there—but of course the landlady of the pub wasn't present to receive them, and it was Maia, moreover, who had discovered the body and alerted the police. It would seem churlish not to attend her exhibition, if only to congratulate her. Between 6 and 8 pm the crowd of viewers grew to the point where Maia began to wonder if the barn could hold many more. As she moved around the space she couldn't help hearing in the hum of conversation words and phrases crackling with human interest, *tueur*, *victime*, *violence*; at the same time, people were in fact looking at the paintings, she did receive praise, and several little red stickers declaring 'I am sold' appeared on paintings through the course of the evening. So the event could only be called a success.

Next morning the police came to interview her—two men, one in uniform and the other in plain clothes. The three of them crowded round the kitchen table. The plain-clothes man did most of the talking. He seemed very keen to know how much of the body she had seen, whether anything above the legs was visible—in particular whether she'd been able to make out the face.

'I thought he was face down in the water? That's what Vincent said.'

But her own description of the soles of the shoes, toes pointing upwards, showed that Vincent had been wrong. She realised it as soon as she'd said it. In any case she hadn't seen the face, no. 'Is it known who it was?'

That was a question the policeman or detective or whatever he was had been asked several times already. Leaning back in his chair, one huge hand upon the tablecloth, he recited a non-committal formula of professional agnosticism. Soon after that they left.

'Course they know who it is,' said Dave Gibbard propping up the bar that lunchtime. 'But they're not going to give away sensitive information when they're still scurrying around looking for incriminating evidence, are they.'

'Surely if they gave out the man's name people might come forward with evidence?' said Maia.

'Too sensitive,' he replied darkly.

'What d'you mean, sensitive?' demanded Brian. In one hand he held a gin and tonic while with his other hand he scooped peanuts from a bowl on the counter.

'I mean politically sensitive.'

'Oo la la,' commented George, eyebrows aloft.

'Dave's got a theory, haven't you Dave?' said Brian. 'Go on then, tell us your theory. Identity of victim, motive of killer, method of . . .'

'Steak frites?' It was Béatrice, pink and dishevelled. Brian pushed the bowl of peanuts away to make space and George leant over to Dave and said, 'This will keep him quiet. Now continue.'

'Well, isn't it obvious who it might be?' Dave seemed to be enjoying himself.

'No it isn't,' said Brian through a mouthful of chips.

'The missing scientist, of course. The chap who went AWOL a week ago, the one who was giving evidence to the virology committee—Leblanc was his name. He was probably a marked man as soon as he accepted the commission.'

'Marked by whom?'

'Either side. It depends which way he was leaning.'

'And which way was he leaning?' asked Maia.

'We won't know till they publish the report in three months' time or whenever.' Dave sounded almost gleeful.

That afternoon Maia decided to go into St Hilaire, Fournhac's only church, to light a candle for the soul of the dead man. She had a couple of hours before Julius was due to arrive. The church was a fourteenth century building with a squat tower overlooking a small square, the Place de l'Église, around which huddled a few pastel-coloured houses, the post office and a hairdresser's. In the middle of the square stood the war memorial, topped by the figure of a walrus-moustached soldier advancing with bayonetted rifle. A pigeon perched peacefully on his helmet. On three of the stone column's four sides were carved the names of the fallen dead from two world wars: a bushel from the Second World War, a whole harvest from the Great War. Maia often paused before this monument on her way to church. She would read over some of the names to herself, names which frequently repeated themselves: a trio of Gilberts, a quartet of Bouchers. Such a cluster of surnames could represent a local family's full complement of males, all swept away by November 1918. Standing in front of the memorial Maia would close her eyes and offer a prayer for the dead; once inside the church she might light a candle. Today she didn't pause by the memorial but walked straight on. Whoever he was, however he had died, somebody must mourn him. No doubt his family would be contacted as soon as his identity was established—maybe they had already been contacted—but the idea of a human being lying forgotten and uncherished in a morgue even for twenty-four hours was horrible to her.

Entering the cool dim church from the sunlit square, Maia as always felt the world dropping away behind her. She passed underneath the west gallery and stopped by the ancient stone font. The church was empty of life. Absurd statement! This was God's dwelling-place; unless your spirit was muffled, unless you were so tightly swaddled in Self as to be deaf and blind, how could you not sense His breathing, albeit each breath was as an aeon, each heartbeat the lifetime of a sun? In the avenue of poplars God might whisper and beckon, but in this church—in any church—he was actually present, he sat upon his throne that you might approach him on bended knee. That was the meaning of the Eucharist.

She moved down the body of the church towards the altar. Just in front of the chancel steps, over to one side, was a candle holder, a matrix of open-mouthed cylinders into which the devout could insert candles taken out of an adjacent box. (A voluntary donation of a few euros was suggested.) Two candles were already burning and, lighting a taper from one of these, Maia took a third from the box and touched its wick with the flame. A new brightness was kindled; she fixed the candle in place and stepped back a couple of paces.

St Hilaire was a small church but rich in representation. Behind the altar table, on which stood a vase of fading flowers, was a painting of Christ on the cross, and to either side of it were statues, one of Saint Hilary himself, the other of Our Lady. The doctor of the church was clothed in the rich vestments befitting a fourth-century bishop; a simple blue robe draped the figure of God's mother. Maia looked into the calm and loving face and addressed her prayer to Mary, Queen of Heaven. It was to Mary that she generally prayed—Mary the intercessor, who brings our petitions before God and pleads our case for us. Maia hadn't known the dead man, any more than she'd known the Gilberts and the Bouchers of Fournhac. But she knew that he was a human being and had lived a human life. He would need God's mercy like everyone else, whether he had died by his own hand or by another's, or if he had simply slipped on a wet log and cracked his skull on a rock. Suicide, murder, accident: these were things for the police to investigate, for coroners to determine. But every child needs a parent's love.

Mary mother of God, mother of us all, bless us with your love, take us to your bosom, cradle us.

'I'm your mother now.' The woman with the straight hair and thick glasses stands over Maia smiling at her. Maia knows it isn't true. Her real mother is somewhere else but she's still her mother. You can't stop being someone's mother, except perhaps by dying. 'You're my foster mother.' 'That's the same thing.' 'No it isn't.' Whereupon the woman hits her.

Holy Mary, virgin pure, blessed art thou among women and blessed is the fruit of thy womb Jesus, O mother mild, O heavenly mother mild.

'I want to see my real mother.' 'The woman you're talking about is not your mother.' 'Yes she is, she is…' Maia is curled up in a ball on the bed, sobbing. 'She's my mother.' 'She's dead now. The woman you're talking about is dead.' 'She isn't…' 'She is dead.'

Mary mother Mary pray for us sinners, do not desert your children, do not desert, pray for us now and at the hour of our, at the hour of our . . . pray for us Mary.

Maia opened her eyes. Three flames danced before her—they bobbed and danced, blurry and bright. Her mother had fled, fled away into the shadows.

*

'That coffee smells good.'

He stood in the doorway, hands in his dressing gown pockets, hair rumpled, the same pallor on his face as yesterday.

'It's freshly made. Did you sleep well?'

Julius came into the room. Maia pulled out a chair for him and he sat down on it heavily.

'Like a log. What time is it?'

She pointed to the clock on the wall.

'Goodness—gone ten. Have you been up long? Oh, you've been to the boulangerie and back . . .'

'If you want I could fry you up some eggs and bacon?'

'No, no, I can only face croissants for breakfast. And similar forms of carbohydrate. At the hotel they lay on a kind of smorgasbord, ham, cheese, cereal, pickles, the works. I don't know how anyone can cope with such variety first thing in the morning.' He took a pain au chocolat onto his plate. 'It's not healthy.'

Maia poured out the coffee. She took a bag of white sugar off a shelf and placed it next to Julius's mug with a teaspoon then sat down opposite him.

He gave her a wan smile. 'Dear friend, you remember everything.'

'I remember you have sugar in your coffee. There's plenty I forget.'

He accepted the morsel of consolation along with the sugar. Yes, we all forget things, especially as we get older. Nothing to worry about. Some are more forgetful than others, that's all: it's a matter of degree. And sometimes things do come back to you, gratuitously. You might be caused to recollect something by a quite arbitrary image, like a blue hoarding, or the bridge with figures on it in a willow pattern . . .

'Was there a dead body in the river, then?' he asked. 'Or was it a trick of the light or something? Somehow I couldn't square the idea of a floating corpse with sleepy little Fournhac.'

'Yes, there was a body, the body of a man. They've removed it now. I got interviewed by the police yesterday.'

'They think you dunnit?'

Maia laughed. 'They wanted to know if I'd seen the face. Which I hadn't. Why do you think they asked that, though? They'll have seen the face for themselves. Anyway, one of the expats who comes to the pub thinks the dead man must have been the scientist who went missing a while ago. He'd been giving evidence to a planning committee.'

'I can see that might make a person feel suicidal.'

('He's a droll fellow, our Julius,' Johnny said to her once. 'Drollery usually conceals something.' She'd found the remark far-fetched at the time.)

'But do you *know* about this plan, Julius? This plan to build a big research lab in the forests over near Valliguières?'

'The virology institute? Yes, Philippe told me about it. The scientist you're talking about—is the idea that...'

'Dave Gibbard thinks he was killed before he could say too much.'

'And do you believe that?'

'I've no idea. But Julius...' She looked suddenly desperate. 'They want to build it in the middle of our forest. The forest where your dukes went hunting. Isn't it terrible? Don't you think that it's terrible?'

'It's very terrible.' He spoke as if from a great distance. 'And we must... we will... I...'

These lands belong to the Duchy of Uzès. You may not build here. The ancient rights and privileges of our family, bestowed on us by the gracious kindness of the monarch -

'Ferro non auro.'

'What?'

'By iron, not by gold. It's our motto. The family motto. *Iron.* My family has always relied on the strength of arms to achieve its goals, never on bribery or riches, that's for other families, you know the sort I mean, wasters and toadies. We will fight to protect our rights. Do you hear? We will *fight.*' He stood up and the chair behind him fell backwards onto the floor with a clatter. 'Fight with whatever weapons we have, which might be guns or explosives or words or—or the Dark Web. I will write a pamphlet.' He stared at her. There was panic in his eyes. 'A pamphlet,' he croaked. 'And I... I...' Congestion, struggle. Jaws grinding, grinning grinding, grinning jaws grinding—'I *defy* you!' he yelled at last.

Maia came round the table and picked the chair up from off the floor. She took Julius by the elbow and looking into her face with frightened eyes he lowered himself onto the seat.

'Julius, you haven't finished your coffee. Look. And would you like another pastry? How about another pastry?'

He nodded. 'Yes, that would be nice.'

Maia put an almond croissant on his plate. He regarded it—it was as if he was considering what sort of thing it might be. A moment later his hands went to his temples, first the right hand and then the left, but they didn't stay there; he returned them to the table, palms down on either side of his plate, equidistant, neat. His left hand was trembling.

'Maia,' he said, 'I have the beginnings of a headache. I should probably take something for it.'

'I can get you an aspirin . . .'

'And I should take my Alethex. The little yellow pill.' He appeared puzzled. 'Three times a day—I haven't taken it already, have I?'

'Not since you came downstairs. Did you perhaps take it in your bedroom?'

'In my bedroom . . .'

He looked at his croissant. 'In my bedroom,' he repeated.

After breakfast Julius had a shower and got dressed. Maia suggested they walk up to the barn; it was another sunny day and they could stop half way at the memorial garden from where one had a view over the valley with wooded hills in the distance. It had been a favourite place for them to sit and talk in the old days, the period when Julius was recovering from his catastrophe, his first catastrophe. Johnny had left the year before but they didn't talk so much of that. Maia still thought then that Johnny might come back, that perhaps he would even arrive while Julius was staying in Fournhac so that the three of them could revive their earlier friendship, relive the good times. Slip back into Eden by a side gate.

'Why has Johnny gone off like this?' Julius asked her one evening back then. They were walking home from the cemetery. Julius had been curious to see it; he liked to wander among the headstones and memorials which line the streets of a rural French necropolis, names and dates giving glimpses of past lives, buried sorrows. He had enjoyed Fournhac's, which he declared 'very characteristic'.

'I suppose he got bored,' replied Maia. 'Bored with the routine, bored with the peace and quiet.' Bored with me, she added to herself.

'How could anyone get bored living here? It's too lovely. And what about you? Does he think he can just up sticks and leave you? Without even an explanation?'

Johnny could certainly think such a thing, as it turned out. Oh yes, he could think it for a good twenty years.

Now as they set off from *Les Pêcheurs* her mind went back to that period. Although the rationale for Julius's trip lay in a personal tragedy Maia looked back on his sojourn with her as something precious—life lived in a state of heightened consciousness. For six weeks he had stayed under her roof while she nursed him out of his depression and put him back on his feet. She had got to know him well; if the soul is a house, she had been all around it, had been shown all the cupboards in corners and all the hidden stairways. Then at the end of the six weeks it was: off you go now, look after yourself, keep in touch. Become a famous writer. I'll be fine. And hadn't she been fine? The sky continued blue, the birds still sang in the air. She had been fine.

They were crossing the stone bridge. A tractor came up behind them and they went in single file on the narrow pavement until it had passed, then got back onto the road. The tractor growled up the hill ahead of them, up the main street that led to M. Bouvet's barn. It was a weekday morning and there weren't many people about. Some way up the street a figure emerged from the boulangerie holding a bag with a pair of baguettes sticking out of it. The figure crossed the road and disappeared into an alley.

'It's just the same,' said Julius. 'It hasn't changed at all.'

'They've built some new houses on the outskirts but otherwise you're right. Fournhac doesn't change much. It's a small French country town.'

'I can see my past here,' he said. 'I mean, this road, these houses—they are literally my past. I could close my eyes and try to remember them, as I used to try to remember them back in London, but I don't need to, do

I? I just have to open my eyes and look and there they are. They're the same houses I vaguely and uncertainly recalled, or merely imagined, sitting in my office in KCL. The very same. But how clear and present they are to sight!'

He looked at her and his eyes were shining. He is cheerful, she thought, he has forgotten this morning.

'A joke, of sorts,' he went on. 'The eyes see so much better than the mind. Or: you can remember better with your eyes open. That's true, isn't it, and so is: you can see better with your memory. How different it is to look upon a familiar face than an unfamiliar one—you perceive all sorts of things written there, there's so much meaning and character in the person's expression, so much lies behind it. The same with a building or a street. It could even be a building which you come across for the first time. If you know its history, if you know how its past connects with other pasts, with all the comings and goings of men and women alive or dead, and if your knowledge is itself something with deep roots in you, something that has grown gradually over the years, layers and accretions of historical truth adding depth and yet more depth until the building whose threshold you finally cross, passing through the wicket gate into the shady courtyard, itself seems to be a living breathing creature—then the face of that building will be as dear and familiar to you as the face of an old friend. And the man who orders its demolition will seem to you a murderer.'

He wasn't sure if he said all this or only thought it. It hardly mattered. The thoughts were true, that was what mattered. Maia would sense what he meant. She had probably been thinking the very same thoughts. It became clear to him that they must have been think-ing them simultaneously. That indeed would be only natural.

They had arrived at the memorial garden. Julius walked past the box hedges, around the central plinth and over to the low wall beyond which the vista spread itself. Maia came and stood beside him. Down in the valley the river snaked its way through fields, skirted the foot of the garden which sloped down from *Les Pêcheurs* and disappeared beneath the stone arches of the bridge. A glint of sunlight beyond the bridge showed it con-tinuing on its way, winding between oaks and willows towards the ruined water mill.

It's flowing towards Valliguières, thought Maia.

*

'Over from Blighty, are you? And where are you staying? In one of the local gites?'

Brian Decker was supporting himself on the bamboo cane he took with him on his strolls: classic design with a chestnut crook handle. On his head was a panama hat with a red band. For some reason he was wearing a bow tie.

'Julius is staying with me,' said Maia. 'He's driven over from Uzès.'

'Ah, lovely Uzès. The gem of Languedoc. Have you been before?'

'A number of times,' said Julius.

'Julius is an expert on the history of the duchy,' put in Maia.

'An expert, eh? I suppose you're a university man? Never went to college myself. My wife did—she was a Girton girl. They had a joke about Girton women...'

'We're just going up to the barn. I thought I'd show Julius my paintings. There's one of him, actually.'

She began to move. Brian stepped aside for them, courteous as always.

'Nice to meet you,' he said as Julius followed in Maia's wake. They had only gone a few yards when Brian called after them: 'Oh, but have you heard the news? You might have trouble getting back, you know.'

Julius turned and said, 'I beg your pardon?'

'Getting back where?' asked Maia.

'Getting back to England. They're grounding planes. It's those Rebex people. Credible threats, apparently. You might want to check with your airline.'

Maia and Julius looked at one another. 'Stranded in Languedoc, what a fate,' he smiled.

'Of course it could all blow over,' Brian pronounced over his shoulder as he made off down the hill.

The barn door was open when they arrived. Maia thought she had taken care to close it the previous evening but it had been a long day and she was tired and distracted when she cleared up and turned off the lights some time after eleven. Easily done, and anyway the door had no lock. They went inside; everything was just as she'd left it.

'Oh, *yes*,' exclaimed Julius, 'what a great venue.'

'Do you think so?'

'Much better than one of those chi-chi London galleries you'd pay an arm and a leg to hire. Is it attached to the farm? The one run by old whatsisname? Bouvet?'

'Julius, you *do* remember things.'

He was wandering about the barn taking the place in, looking up into the rafters and breathing in the earthy woody smell. His hands were in his pockets and his hair, still wet from the shower, was slicked back on his head— like the young Brahms, thought Maia, and at once she was in an east Oxford kitchen with the waning October light falling on the features of a recent acquaintance, fresh and new and interesting. From a life-drawing class to Coco's to her kitchen he came. She had wondered if the next stop might be her bedroom, played with the idea, half-planned it . . . But that was one of the roads not taken. Down that road there was no Johnny, no Toni, no Paul. Paul's ghostly half-brother or half-sister might be there, the possibility of a possibility. Maia expelled the thought, gently pushed it away.

Julius had come to a standstill in front of a landscape—swirling blues and greens, a bit Van Gogh.

'The road going north out of town past the riding school,' he said. 'Is that still there?'

'No, it went a while ago. There are horses in the field, though. And old Vincent who used to run it, he's still going strong.'

'It's a nice painting. I'd like to buy it.'

'Julius, you don't have to . . .'

'I want to. Can I put a red sticker on it?'

'Why don't you come over here and look at this painting first? You might want to buy it instead.'

'Can't I have both?'

He went over to where she was standing. And here it was, the window onto his past, the forty-year-old portrait. Young fogey in a cravat. Graduate student with rear reflection. Ceci n'est pas un vieillard. Or: Ceci n'est pas encore un vieillard.

'The big kitchen,' he said. 'The Aga stove. Caleb the cat.'

'Yes.'

'If you can part with it, I'd like to buy this too.'

'Of course—I was hoping you'd take it. But you don't have to pay me for it, Julius. Really.'

He shook his head as at a tiresome joke. 'I want to look at some of the others now. I'll come back to these in a moment—' The gesture encompassed sun and moon, sprawling Billy and the Annunciation, 'but first show me something of Johnny. You must have some pictures of Johnny.'

Maia took him over to a painting she had done of Johnny in the month before he disappeared, sitting at the desk in the upper room of the pub, looking out of the dormer window. A yellow Post-it note was attached to the lower bar of the picture frame reading *Pas à Vendre*. Julius took off his glasses to clean the lenses, returned them to his nose and sighed.

'I wonder where the silly fool is now.'

Maia didn't answer. She was remembering those sittings, usually in the mornings straight after breakfast. Johnny had seemed calm and happy. It was springtime, there were some starlings nesting under the eaves of the roof.

'I'll show you another,' she said.

Julius followed her down the barn to where the charcoal nude hung. 'This is a much earlier one. Johnny had just got out of the bath ...' She stopped suddenly. Julius saw it at the same time. 'Why ...' he began.

The picture was hanging upside down. In this orientation it was hard to interpret the lines and shapes. Johnny's feet were clearest, emerging from an ambiguous mass and kicking the air. Julius waited for her explanation. Eventually Maia said: 'It'll be the children. The Bouvet children. They must have slipped in early this morning before going to school.' She was re-hanging the picture the right way up. 'It's just a joke, a prank.'

'It's not a very funny joke,' said Julius.

'They're only young.'

It's half an hour before opening and Maia is standing behind the bar reading a novel. From the front door comes a loud knocking. She glances at her watch, puts the open book face down on the counter and goes to open the door. There's no one there: she stands in the porch looking out onto an empty road. 'Hello?' she calls. Silence. A body falls from the sky and lands on its feet in front of her. 'Hello!' yells Johnny, grabbing her in an embrace.

'Got onto the porch canopy from our bedroom window,' he tells her later. 'Good joke, eh?'

'You scared me,' she says. 'Prankster.'

He grins back at her impenitent.

VI

IN 1565, LETTERS PATENT ISSUED by Charles IX of France elevated the viscounty of Uzès to the status of a duchy. Seven years later the dukes of Uzès were made members of the French peerage, their rank being directly below that of the princes of the blood. The family's rise in the world was to continue: in 1632, upon the beheading for treason of the last Duke of Montmorency, the title of First Duke of France was transferred to Uzès, bringing with it both the duty of defending in combat the honour of the queen mother and the right of pronouncing the words 'Le roi est mort. Vive le roi!' at the funeral of every French king.

The first member of the house of Crussol to be associated with Uzès had been Jacques de Crussol, eighth viscount, whose marriage to Simone d' Uzès in 1486 effected the joining of the houses of Uzès and Crussol and the merging of their coats of arms into one: per bale barry of six or and vert, and gules, three bendlets or. The grandson of Simone and Jacques, Antoine, was a Protestant military leader whose pacification of

Bas-Languedoc, Provence and Dauphiné during the wars of religion earned for him the favour of the Catholic king Charles IX and for his family the duchy, as we have seen. It is thought that his wife's influence at court helped to oil the wheels. Antoine's great-grandson Henri, fourth duke of Uzès, a Renaissance man in his way, cultivated and athletic, corresponded with the playwright Jean Racine, who briefly visited Uzès in 1661-2, some years before fame came to him as the author of *Phèdre* and *Andromaque*. Presumably the two men became acquainted during this visit. A portion of their correspondence has survived; it proved a crucial source for the young historian Julius Durward when he was writing a life of Henri de Crussol in the 1990s. Particularly touching are those letters, written near the end of his too short life, in which Henri le duc records the grief he felt when his beloved daughter Cécile died aged eight, of what doctors now think was meningitis. 'My life has become a burden to me,' writes the duke in Durward's English translation, 'and I look for solace in the forgetfulness induced by wine. There is a door in the palace which I can no longer walk past, the door of her room. I pray to God…'

'What's that shiny thing hanging up there in a sort of cage?' said Kelly.

Travis looked up from his guidebook to where Kelly was pointing.

'I think it's a bell.'

'I wonder how they ring it,' said Kelly. 'I can't see a rope.'

The two of them were standing in the Rue Amiral de Brueys in the shadow of the duchy's massive walls. Kelly had her back to the duchy and was gazing up at the Tour de l'Évêque, between which and its sister tower, the Tour de l'Évêche, ran the Rue Entre les Deux Tours, invisible to Kelly. Much indeed is invisible to the pedestrian in Uzès, with its narrow streets and tall buildings. Kelly and Travis, she in a light summer dress, he in a t-shirt and shorts, had been wandering round the town since mid-morning, having eaten a leisurely breakfast at their hotel. They had yet to stumble upon the open and breezy Place aux Herbes, where at this moment Julius Durward was reading a newspaper and enjoying a pre-prandial Pernod.

'Shall we take a look at the chateau?' said Travis. 'It's where Durward's duke lived, the one who makes an appearance in *Pandora's Mirror*.'

'All part of the assignment—sounds good to me.'

They walked down the street and round into the Place du Duché. The entrance to the duchy came into view on their left—an arched gateway set well back from the road with a pediment supported by columns and a wicket gate. Cars were parked with their noses to the duchy walls.

'Two tickets for inside the chateau, please,' Travis said to the woman at the kiosk by the wicket gate.

'Deux billets,' translated Kelly. 'S'il vous plaît.'

Inside the castle were artworks, relics and memorabilia dating from the middle ages up to the present day. Ornate furniture, antlers mounted on walls, a huge Aubusson tapestry, paintings and photographs of dukes and duchesses; Kelly imagined herself moving through some labyrinthine stage set. Where were the actors? She supposed that she and Travis were the actors, playing themselves of course, other members of the cast including those Japanese ladies and that middle-aged man wearing a baseball cap. But as well as the actors there must be ghosts, the ghosts of the men and women whose portraits looked down on them with the air more of observers than of observed. They witnessed the steady stream of intruders and held fast to their less ephemeral reality.

'Here's a character,' said Travis standing before the framed black and white photograph of an old lady in front of a car with enormous wheels. 'This is Marie Adrienne Anne Victurnienne Clémentine de Rochechouart de Mortemart, duchess of Uzès from 1872 to 1878.' He turned a page in his guidebook. 'She was President of the French Automobile Club in the 1920s and a poet, novelist, historian, painter and sculptor.'

'She looks like she's just eaten a lemon.'

'Her grandma founded the Veuve Clicquot brand.'

'What's that?'

'Champagne.'

'I'm for grandma.' Kelly looked up at a painting of a woman in a hat wearing a fur which seemed to have slipped off her shoulders. 'Is that her? The motoring duchess?'

Travis consulted his guidebook. 'Yes, that's her. How did you know?'

'It's nineteenth century. No lemon in that one.'

Kelly considered the life of an aristocratic woman of those times and wondered if she'd have enjoyed it. A lot would depend on your husband and whether you could stand him. Marriage was marriage in the 1870s, a bit on the side was frowned on if you were female and contraception was primitive. Maybe the duke was a lovely guy. In any case, if the duchess stopped duchessing in 1878 that probably meant she was a widow for most of her career, which will have made room for all that writing and driving. Not a bad arrangement all things considered.

They made their way through a couple of doorways into what appeared to be a dining room. A table in the centre was laid for eight places, with two candlesticks and some bowls of fake fruit filling in the spaces. The chairs had been lined up against a wall, high-backed and upholstered in green; above them hung the Aubusson tapestry, depicting a confused scene of figures in, or falling out of, a boat rowed by a cross-looking man with a beard—Alexander the Great as it turned out. On the walls to either side of the tapestry were a number of hunting trophies.

'So did Julius Durward sniff around here?' asked Kelly. 'I guess he must have. D'you think he ever sat on one of these chairs? They could have a plaque: *Julius Durward's bum was . . .*'

'Kelly.' There was irritation in his voice. 'Come on.'

'Sorry, Trav. Is JD off limits? Naughty Kelly.' She slapped her wrist.

Travis sighed. 'He's a real human being and we're going to be meeting him in person in a couple of hours. He wrote quite an important book, I hope you don't mention his bum.'

'Don't authors *have* bums?'

'No they don't, not for present purposes.' He turned away. Kelly, apparently for her own benefit, raised her eyebrows and shoulders in a gesture of mystification. She followed him out of the room. 'Pardon, pardon,' apologised one of the Japanese ladies as they narrowly avoided colliding with one another. Travis had stopped half way down the wood-panelled corridor. His attention was on a small oil painting of a man with a pointed beard reminiscent of Charles I of England. The corridor was dimly lit and one had to peer quite close to make out the man's features.

'Who's this?' Kelly asked.

'Henri de Crussol. It's the only surviving portrait of him. Painted the year before he died.'

The couple stood side by side, arms touching. Kelly's eyes and the duke's eyes met. It seemed to her that he held her in his gaze and that in those eyes were questioning and pain, appealing to her and reaching out to her across the centuries.

*

He was feeling better today. Yesterday his mind had wandered rather. He vaguely recalled saying some odd stuff over breakfast, and in the afternoon Maia had dissuaded him from swimming in the river. The water had looked so inviting from the parapet of the bridge. He had to admit that it wasn't quite the trip to Fournhac he'd envisaged, not quite the happy reunion he'd been looking forward to. Poor Maia, she had done her best. She'd fed and watered him, taken him around the town, introduced him to people. Once or twice she'd shed some tears, but then Maia was a woman of deep feelings, sentimental even, and seeing him again had probably put her in mind of Johnny and of the good old days. Whenever they were. When were they? Oxford nineteen-eighty-something was when they were, when Caleb the cat roamed the kitchen and a trio of friends cycled round the Oxfordshire lanes together. Et in Arcadia ego, and not a cloud in the sky. On the horizon, very distant, there was a grey cloud and slowly, very slowly, it was approaching. But in Oxford in nineteen-eighty-something it was invisible. Sufficient unto the day was the evil thereof. He and Maia could both remember the evil, that was part of the problem, it stood between them and they didn't speak of it as they had spoken of it when he first visited Fournhac, except fleetingly and with a light touch. It was a long time ago: natural to think that the wound was less raw now. And Maia would be concerned not to overload him, not to put pressure on too many sore places. In some ways he was just one big bruise. Mad to boot.

However, today he was feeling better. Perhaps the Alethex was finally kicking in. He took another sip of Pernod and turned the page of his newspaper, placing a water jug on top of it to stop it blowing about in the breeze. It seemed they were grounding planes. One explosive device had already been discovered. Well, if he were forced to extend his trip, so be it. He could always go by ferry but the things made him seasick, and as for the channel tunnel, tickets these days cost the earth—he would insist on charging it to the department if Hugh started nagging him about the date of his return. Hugh might just have to be patient. Julius looked up from his newspaper and let his eyes wander round the square: the plane trees, the fountain, the sober archways. What was it that man had said? *Gem of Languedoc*. The idea of simply staying put was very attractive. If I ended my days here I wouldn't mind at all, no, I wouldn't mind one little bit.

He glanced at his watch. In an hour and a half he had to be back at the hotel to receive Mr Travis Beggs with a view to discussing with him the possibility of giving an inaugural lecture for the Optimex Foundation. The appointment was written on the back of his hand so was perfectly definite. The hand is a primary text. He raised his text in the air to attract the attention of the waitress. When she arrived at his table he asked her for the menu; the girl nodded and went off to get him one. Julius finished his Pernod.

*

'He doesn't look very old. What did he die of?'

'He fell off some wall. Or threw himself—they're not sure which. It was near the cathedral.'

'Why would he throw himself off a wall?' Kelly addressed her question to the portrait as much as to Travis. Perhaps the eyes could tell her.

'He seems to have been a depressive. Or depressed. In his letters he sounds that way. His daughter died of meningitis. But it could just have been that he got drunk on the local wine and tripped or fell.'

'He might have got drunk because he was depressed.'

'Uh-huh.'

The mute face looked out at them from the canvas. Far behind the millimetre-thick image, in a dimension they couldn't access, lay the secret of the duke's pain. Kelly felt herself trying to penetrate it, reach through to it.

Travis took hold of her hand. 'Come on, let's go. We should grab a bite to eat somewhere.'

'I don't think he looks like a depressive.'

'Come on.'

Together they left the duke behind and wandered out of the chateau in search of lunch. They bought a couple of filled baguettes and ate them sitting on a bench on the Boulevard Gambetta. Three or four pigeons flew down to join them. The Boulevard Gambetta is a relatively busy road, being in fact none other than the D979. Cars and even lorries drove past.

'I'll need to get changed at the hotel,' said Travis. 'This is a suit and tie job.'

'Do I have to get changed?'

'No, you look fine. You look great. You always look great.'

'But do I look *appropriate*?'

'For a cokehead you look as respectable as an archbishop.'

'Which archbishop did you have in mind?'

He turned round on the bench and kissed her on the lips.

'I'm eating!' she protested. A pigeon jumped up beside her and without looking she batted it away. Eventually she finished her baguette and they made their way back to the hotel. In their room Travis put on his suit and tie while Kelly checked her phone for messages sitting cross-legged by the open French windows whose flimsy curtains danced in the breeze.

'Say, Trav,' she called. He was in the bathroom adjusting his tie in front of the mirror.

'Yeah?'

'I'm just reading the news and it says that flights out are being cancelled because of the terror threat.'

He came back into the room, both hands on the knot of his tie.

'What? Really?'

'Really really. We might have to stay in Uzès. Till they're up and running again.'

'Fuck.'

'Yeah, we could do that. And look around the town.'

'I'll have to get in touch with Uncle Harry. He's paying for this trip.' Travis was putting on his jacket. 'Gives us longer to persuade the professor, I guess.'

'And longer to get on his nerves. Speaking of nerves, Trav, how are we feeling? Ready to encounter a world-famous brainbox? Fired up for the charm offensive?'

'I'm counting on you for that,' he said, offering her a hand. She took it and pulled herself to her feet.

'I haven't prepared,' she said.

'How d'you mean?'

'I should have looked at his book, shouldn't I.'

'It'll be something for you to read if we get stuck in Uzès. Better than airport fiction.'

Julius was sunk in one of the black leather armchairs when the couple walked through the hotel doors at 2.07 p.m. The neatly dressed young man, clean-shaven and short-haired, was turning his head from side to side but the blonde girl in a cotton dress the colour of double cream had already spotted him and she nudged her companion and pointed. Now they were walking towards him, the boy smiling stiffly, the girl a couple of steps behind. Julius struggled to his feet.

'Professor Durward?' said Travis, right hand thrust forward.

'That's me,' replied Julius, submitting to the handshake. He turned to Kelly. 'Mrs Beggs?'

'Kelly,' she smiled, and they too shook hands.

For a few moments the three of them stood around. Kelly broke the silence.

'Travis, I know you two have a lot to talk about. I can go and amuse myself if you'll lend me your guidebook.'

'Oh no,' said Julius, 'you're very welcome to stay, Miss—Kelly. We're all on holiday, aren't we? Pleasure as well as business.'

'Absolutely,' concurred Travis.

'Well then,' Julius went on. 'Why don't we get out of this lobby to start with? How about a stroll by the cathedral? It has a wonderful campanile, rather like a miniature Tower of Pisa. The rest of the building is nineteenth century, while inside are some…' He trailed off. 'Follow me, won't you,' he finished, and started for the exit. Travis and Kelly obeyed.

As they walked to the cathedral Julius talked, more or less at random, of the history of Uzès, of the Occitan language, of local food and wine. Occasionally his talk became a mumble. Kelly glanced at Travis and read uncertainty in his face. So this was the author of *Pandora's Mirror*. To all appearances he had a screw loose.

They came to the cathedral and standing before its beige-stoned façade Julius at last fell silent. 'Fantastic,' said Travis. A few yards off a woman with dark glasses and a lipsticky smile was frozen in an attitude of warm-blooded ease having her photo taken by a friend with the cathedral as backdrop. Kelly's eyes scanned the shapes and shadows of the building. There were strong vertical lines, circular windows, two figures occupying niches to either side of the entrance.

'It's dedicated to St Theodoritus, a fourth-century martyr.' Julius was moving to the right. The couple moved with him. 'One of Julian the Apostate's men put him to death for not yielding up the church treasures. A greedy lot, the Romans; not content with taxing the natives they were inclined to top up their coffers with loot. You'd need a compulsory purchase order for that nowadays. Still, you could say that Theodoritus had the last laugh insofar as he had a cathedral named after him, which the emperor Julian's bully-boy never did—whatever his name was. I think it might have been Julian too.' He laughed. 'I don't mean Julian *two*, of course. Julian *too*. Not that you can hear the difference, am I being obscure?' He threw an unexpectedly sharp glance at Travis.

'Obscure? No, sir . . . not . . . I think I'm following you.'

'Good. Well anyway. Here's the campanile. Known as the Tour Fenestrelle, on account of the pierced stonework. Piercing like windows. The sky visible beyond, depending on your angle of vision. And as we walk along this side of the cathedral we approach, ladies and gentlemen, one of the curiosities of Uzès, a commemorative building somewhat resembling a public convenience but which would prefer to be known as a pavilion—there it is ahead of us.'

'With the dome?' said Kelly.

'With the dome. The low wall which defines the edge of the cathedral precinct is as you see interrupted by this small but perfectly formed edifice, half of which lies within the precinct and half without, it having originally been built to replace a tower, a piece of mediaeval fortification from which the armies of those hostile to Uzès could be repulsed.'

Kelly thought: he's lecturing us because lecturing's what he's used to and it puts him at his ease. He is a sad man as well as nervy.

They had arrived at the pavilion. Travis went to stand by the low wall abutting it. He surveyed the landscape, thickly-wooded hills in the middle distance, a blue-grey horizon beyond—above it all the burnished sky. Kelly joined him. She looked down over the knee-high wall at the rocking trees below. The mistral was reviving.

'Did Henri de Crussol fall off this wall?' she asked as Julius came up.

'He did. To his death. You know about the fourth duke?'

'We saw his portrait in the chateau.'

'I was reading to Kelly from my guidebook,' put in Travis.

'And you told me he's mentioned in *Pandora's Mirror*, Trav, remember?'

Travis looked embarrassed and began to say something but Julius said, 'I'm pleased you've read my book, Mr Beggs—otherwise I'd worry that you were letting yourself in for a pig in a poke.'

'Sir?'

'You need to have *some* idea of the sort of man who'll be inaugurating the Optiflex Institute or whatever it calls itself, no?' Julius lowered himself onto the parapet with his back to the green vista, facing them. His knees jutted out and he rested his hands on the wall to either side of him. 'I suppose your employer chose to invite me on the strength of that book, so I assume he has read it. But he isn't here. You are his representative, his ambassador so to speak. It is appropriate for you to be armed with some knowledge of the person you are to be interviewing—after all it's a very generous emolument I'm being offered, very generous. You need to arrive at an informed opinion about me I would say, before either of us signs on the dotted line. I might be ...'

A jingling erupted in Travis's jacket pocket. He drew out his phone and checked the caller's number.

'Uncle Harry,' he said, moving off with the phone to his ear. Julius raised interrogatory eyebrows.

'It's Mr Selkirk,' explained Kelly.

'Ah. Deus ex machina.'

Travis was pacing up and down under a tree. Every now and then he would gesture with his free hand while he said something; he listened more than he spoke.

'Tell me about this building, Professor Durward,' said Kelly. 'You said it was built to replace a tower.'

Julius stood up. 'It's the Jean Racine Pavilion. You've heard of Racine? He came to Uzès in 1661 on a visit to his uncle. Here's the plaque.' He pointed at a stone rectangle set into the front wall of the pavilion, a couple of feet to the right of a pair of closed doors and the same distance beneath a shuttered window. Kelly read the inscription.

'He was just twenty-two.'

'You know French,' remarked Julius. 'Isn't the quotation at the bottom lovely ... *Et nous avons des nuits plus belles que vos jours.*'

'And here we have nights more beautiful than your days. Yes, it's lovely. Do you think the nights in these parts are as beautiful now as they were then?'

'Why should they have changed?'

She shrugged. 'City noise—light pollution ...'

Julius tilted his head to one side. He was still looking at the plaque. 'Uzès isn't really a city. More of a town, despite having a cathedral. If you've come from London it feels like a village. The gem of Languedoc, someone once called it.'

'Who was that?'

'I forget now. Some writer. Racine and Henri de Crussol exchanged letters, you know.'

'I know.'

Travis was walking towards them. He had finished his phone call.

*

Nico was in the study, listening. Mr Selkirk's voice came to him from the downstairs hallway. He was calling his nephew in France. Nico looked at the clock on the desk in front of him: nearly 9 a.m. Mr Selkirk would be wanting his second cup of coffee presently.

The voice had stopped; the phone call was over. Nico closed the drawer of the desk.

'Nico,' called Mr Selkirk.

He padded out of the room, closing the door behind him, and walked down the parquet-floored corridor towards the stairs.

'Nico?'

'Coming, Mr Selkirk.'

'I'll have my coffee in the library this morning.'

'Yes Mr Selkirk, right away.'

Selkirk heard but did not see Nico coming down the stairs. He was already en route to the library. His conversation with Travis had had a mildly irritating effect on him. It would have been good if this thing could be wrapped up within the week, and here was this damn fool disruption to flights about to drag the whole process out. What did Travis mean by 'ecoterrorists'? Sounded like some kind of publicity stunt, but of course the air companies always erred on the side of safety, they had to. Or had to be seen to. God knew how long it would all last. And getting seats on a train or a boat couldn't be done overnight, quite apart from the extra expense. He was beginning to think that sending the boy over to France had been a pointless luxury. Ideally Travis would make the proposal to Durward, Durward would accept it and Travis would convey the news to his uncle, at which point they could get the ball rolling. But he had a feeling that his PA would relax and lose focus as the duration of his trip stretched out. Young people were like that.

Selkirk made his way over to a bookshelf and picked up a fossil. The cool feel of the stone on the palm of his hand was soothing to his nerves. He could always count on this little trilobite exoskeleton, preserved for half a billion years and as sturdy as ever, to remind him of the sheer power of persistence. He fondled the thing and felt intimations of immortality. If blind mineralization could embalm a creature so perfectly think what cryopreservation could accomplish, designed and guided as it would be by the light of human intelligence. All that was wanted was a suitably fine-tuned nanotechnology...

'Your coffee, Mr Selkirk.'

He replaced the fossil on the shelf and went over to his armchair. Nico had placed the tray on the adjacent table and was standing at a respectful distance.

'Is your nephew well, sir?'

'As well as can be expected,' replied Selkirk, sitting down. 'He's stuck in France, but at least he's made contact with Durward.'

'The English professor?'

'Yes. Apparently Durward's showing him the sights.' He poured some coffee into his cup. 'I hope they don't waste too much time in small talk. This is a business trip, not a holiday. Excellent coffee, Nico,' he added.

'Thank you, sir. Will that be all?'

'Sure. Say, Nico, have you ever been in France?'

'No, sir. Spain is the only country I've visited in Europe.'

'I guess they're pretty similar. The Riviera's not bad. Doreen certainly liked it.'

Nico's nod of agreement covered all possibilities.

*

'It's time to talk business, isn't it. I suggest we accompany our chat with a little wine. How about the Place aux Herbes?'

They were walking back the way they had come, Julius leading.

'I don't think we've been there, have we, Kelly?'

'Not yet.'

'It is the hub of the town,' said Julius, 'its centre of gravity. I think a nice bottle of rosé would be suitable.'

'The Foundation will pay for . . .'

'Please, no—this one's on me. In a sense I'm your host after all. And it was my idea.'

Travis mumbled something.

'That's very kind of you, Professor Durward,' said Kelly.

'Do call me Julius, it saves on breath.' He was walking faster now. His brisker pace seemed in some way to be connected with the escalating wind. Kelly decided to tie her hair back in a ponytail. 'And since you haven't given me your surname it's only fair. But what did your uncle have to say, Mr Beggs? Checking up on you, was he?'

Travis attempted an easy laugh. 'I had to tell him our flight out has been cancelled. He seemed okay with that.'

'I take it your uncle is rich.'

'Yes, sir.'

'He has his own observatory,' said Kelly.

'Is Mr Selkirk of a scientific bent?'

'Absolutely,' said Travis. 'He believes that scientific knowledge is key to improving the lot of humanity. That's what the Optimex Foundation is all about: the future of humanity. That's why we really hope you'll be able to accept our invitation.' He cleared his throat. Julius was looking straight ahead. 'Mr Selkirk thinks highly of your book, sir, as do I. Not that I'm any kind of expert—I studied math at college, not history or politics—but I have read the book a couple of times and you write really—so interestingly about what might be going to happen, about people's ideas of where they're going to . . . and so on.'

'Alexander Selkirk was the original of Robinson Crusoe,' said Julius. 'Now there was a man with survival issues. Very much concerned with the future was Robinson Crusoe, a.k.a. Alexander Selkirk. Scientific knowledge must have been pretty *key* for him, I expect, having to organise his food and shelter on a desert island. Do you think they might be related? Mr Selkirk and Robinson Crusoe, I mean? Is Mr Selkirk waiting for a ship to appear over the horizon to take him away to a better place?'

Travis and Kelly exchanged glances.

'I don't think of the future as a better place myself,' Julius went on. They were coming into the Place aux Herbes. 'But there's no stopping it, is there.'

In the square the branches of the plane trees were swaying in the wind; Travis's tie flapped around till he buttoned up his jacket. The sun disappeared momentarily behind a cloud and the three of them sat down at a table.

'Bouteille de vin rosé, s'il vous plaît,' Julius said to the waiter. 'Have you had lunch?' he asked Kelly.

'Yes, thanks. We ate a couple of baguettes in the Boulevard Gambetta.'

'En plein air.'

'Oui.'

'Your French is good but you're Australian, I think. Is French taught at schools there? I'd have thought Japanese would be more useful.'

'I was home schooled,' said Kelly. 'My mother taught all five of us. She made up the syllabus.'

'Catholic family?'

'Yes.'

'I have a painter friend who's a devout Catholic, living not far from here. She runs a pub. Used to want to be a nun. Then she met an Irishman.' He looked at her carefully. 'She could paint you. She's a good portrait painter, very good.'

Travis coughed.

'I haven't forgotten you, Mr Beggs, have no fear. Ah, here is our wine, just as the sun has come out. Blessed synchrony. A veritable symphony of synchrony... Philippe!'

He was looking open-mouthed past Kelly and she turned and saw a bald man in a black polo-neck jumper coming towards them. He had a grin on his face and dimples in his cheeks. Julius rose from his chair. 'Philippe, you crazy anarchist, where have you sprung up from?' He had grabbed Philippe by the hand and was pumping it. Philippe said something in response then directed his dimpled smile first upon Travis and then more lingeringly upon Kelly.

'I thought I might find you in your hotel, but the receptionist there told me you had gone out and suggested the Place aux Herbes. She said you were more or less a fixture here.'

Julius was pulling up a fourth chair.

'Travis Beggs, pleased to meet you,' said Travis, holding out a hand. Philippe shook it.

'Philippe Arentz, a crazy anarchist friend of the professor's, as you have just heard. But not so crazy. And mademoiselle? ...'

'I'm Kelly,' she answered, and began pouring the rosé into the three glasses.

'Enchanté,' said Philippe, seating himself next to her. Kelly picked up her glass.

'Another glass, we need another glass ...' Julius wandered off in the direction of the bar but the alert waiter was already approaching. The two men met half way and Julius returned with the fourth glass. Flourishing it in the air he placed it in front of his friend and sat down.

'Surely nobody says that any more?' said Kelly.

'What?' asked Travis.

'*Enchanté*. It must be at least a hundred years out of date.'

Philippe, smirking, poured himself some wine with a shaking hand.

'To everyone's good health,' said Julius in a loud voice, raising his glass. 'And to Uzès, the gem of Languedoc.' They all drank.

'I'm very pleased to see you looking so well, Durward. I was concerned for you in Nîmes. We all were.'

'In Nîmes? ... Ah yes. And I am to write you a pamphlet, aren't I. About ... They want to destroy the forest, don't they. They want to build that research centre.'

Philippe turned to Kelly. 'Perhaps you have heard about this. The authorities plan to build a laboratory in the woods not far from here where they can develop new viruses. A terrible scheme. Julius has promised to write about it and condemn it. But tell me'—here he allowed his glance to embrace Travis, 'how do you two come to know Professor Durward? Did you meet in Uzès?'

Travis looked over at Julius. Should he speak for him? No agreement had been come to as yet; the professor might prefer discretion.

'Travis represents an organisation called the Optimex Foundation and he's hoping Julius will give a lecture,' said Kelly. She smiled at Julius and added, 'I think that'd be a gas.'

Philippe said, 'And what is the Optimex Foundation?'

'Over to you, Trav.'

Receiving no hint either way from the professor Travis decided to give his semi-prepared spiel. 'The aim of the Optimex Foundation is simple: to make the world a better place. By channelling the energies of leading intellectuals we can develop global schemes for economic, medical and cultural improvement. The political aspect of the problem will not be ignored. The Foundation will work hand in hand with governmental organisations, as well as with such international bodies as UNESCO and Medecins Sans Frontières. A series of public events...'

'What sorts of improvements?' interrupted Philippe.

'Improvements? Well... tackling disease and poverty; encouraging the development of democratic institutions...'

'Is democracy a *good* thing?'

'As opposed to what, tyranny?'

'Democracy is itself a form of tyranny, I would say. The tyranny of the majority.'

Philippe, looking comfortable, leant back in his chair while Travis bent forward in his, elbows on his knees and hands clasped together beneath the edge of the table. The half empty bottle of rosé stood between them like an umpire. Kelly picked it up and replenished her own glass and Julius's.

'So what's the alternative?' asked Travis.

'You've surely noticed that depends on the historical contingencies of time and place. There is not only one alternative to democracy. Moreover the question is not what particular system of government is found to be operating but whether the governed are free and not in chains. You cannot be free if you are dupes of the system. What is above all necessary is for ordinary people not to regard those who rule them as gods.'

'I don't think...'

'Nor as celebrities, nor as sages, nor as anything more than what they are, which is to say opportunists, apparatchiks and bullies. A hyena eats carrion, a politician gets his sustenance from power over his fellow human beings. He and his minions will jealously defend that power, and in order to do so they will issue those threats which in common parlance are called laws. The laws enable, for example, the destruction of a forest and the creatures that live in it so that servants of the government can create biological weapons under the pretence of—as you put it—"tackling disease". The bare-faced lie and the theft of what belongs to all: those are the hallmarks of the exercise of political power. Backed up, naturally, by lethal force. If the improvement of the human condition is our goal there is only one means to that uncertain end. Resistance.'

Julius started clapping. 'Bravo, Philippe. You excel yourself.'

'I'm sure the director of the Optimex Foundation would be as interested in your views, Mr Aris, as in anyone else's,' said Travis. 'The point is to have as broad a range of approaches and viewpoints as possible. Dialogue between thinkers is always going to be fruitful. Thesis, antithesis...'

'Synthesis!' shouted Julius and Kelly in chorus.

'Hegel was mistaken,' said Philippe. 'Competing political theories are not like ingredients you throw together to make a nice cake. If you throw communism and National Socialism together in the same mixing bowl you get a world war. At least that's what happened last time.'

'We need more wine,' said Julius, beckoning the waiter over.

'Why do you assume the people planning this laboratory want to make biological weapons?' asked Kelly. 'Why assume they have bad motives?'

'Mainly because they are human beings. Also because they are ruthless.'

'In what way?'

Philippe addressed his answer to Julius. 'There is every reason to believe that the virology expert who was submitting evidence to the enquiry and who went missing more than a week ago has been murdered by agents of the state.'

'Maia was telling me about that,' mused Julius. He spoke as if recalling a dream.

'The task of resistance is all the more imperative,' continued Philippe, 'and your assistance, Durward, all the more desirable. I said I would arrange for you to be able to inspect the site. Can you come with me the day after tomorrow? We will need to use your car. The others will be there to give you a guided tour. Max will be among them, a very capable individual.'

'Of course, Philippe, of course.' Julius produced a pen from the inside pocket of his jacket. 'I'll write it on my hand.'

'There's something already there,' said Kelly.

'On my wrist,' corrected Julius.

Travis was extracting a bedraggled insect from his wine glass. 'Is this something to do with Rebex?' he asked flicking it away.

*

Henri had spent the afternoon riding in the woods around Uzès, part of his extensive demesne and a favourite hunting ground of the dukes of Uzès for generations. Today the duke was not hunting, however. He rode alone, it seems, and on his return gave orders that he would not dine but instead would retire to his study. There he meditated or read until some time after midnight, when he left his apartments and was seen quitting the chateau in the direction of the cathedral, his gait unsteady and his demeanour eccentric. A tradition in Uzès states that he fell to his knees outside the cathedral and there offered up a final prayer or lament. He will then have staggered the couple of hundred yards to the low wall which overlooked what in those days was an orchard. His dead body was found among the fruit trees early the next morning. A clear case of suicide would have precluded his burial in consecrated ground but there was sufficient doubt about the matter for the church to allow his interment in the family vault, to lie among the tombs of his ancestors beneath the device which bore their, and his, motto: *Ferro non Auro*. He was just thirty-two.

VII

NICO DID NOT LIKE WHAT he found in Mr Selkirk's desk. He recognised it for what it was: a betrayal. A betrayal releases a man from the obligations that bind him. God will be my judge, said Nico to himself.

He could see Mr Selkirk on the lawn below, standing with his back to the house, his hands clasped behind him. He is contemplating infinity, thought Nico. It is good for him that he does so. Let him contemplate infinity and the state of his soul.

The afternoon sun fell on the desk in front of him and on the documents he had spread out there—deeds, warranties, insurance policies, inventories and valuations, and in the centre of the display, brazen as a hussy, a Last Will and Testament, signed and dated. The date was three weeks ago, the signature Selkirk's. Nico knew that spidery script well. The same signature was appended to another Will with an earlier date on it which he had perused in an altogether different frame of mind some months ago. This document he could not find among the contents of the desk. He had been through all the drawers, this morning and again this afternoon.

Nico looked around the study. Shelves lined the wall opposite the window; on these were arranged a handful of books alongside various knick-knacks. Nico could see no files or folders. His eye ranged along and up, coming to rest on a carriage clock, long silent, which perched alone on the top shelf a few inches from the ceiling. Behind the clock something had been pushed out of sight, a tell-tale corner of it peeping from one edge ... Was it a piece of paper? He pulled the chair that was by his side over to the bookshelves and climbed up onto it. He doubted that he was visible from the lawn but even if he was he could always explain that he'd been swatting a fly or removing a cobweb. With an outstretched hand he fumbled behind the clock and managed to pull out what was there: two sheets of A4 paper, folded. Already he knew that this was unlikely to be what he was looking for but all the same he unfolded the papers and scanned the top page. It was a receipt of payment, for repairs made to the clock in 1997 by one Joshua N. Dalloway, horologist, of Richmond, Virginia. Nico stuffed the document back where it belonged.

He got down from the chair and went back over to the desk. Think, Nico, think! The old man can't have destroyed it. He looked around the study again, slowly, carefully, and this time his eyes lit on an old piano stool which had been exiled from the so-called music room on the occasion of a visiting pianist's having rejected it as too squeaky. The despised stool now stood in a corner of the room beside a standard lamp with a frayed yellow shade, another outcast. Nico stared at the stool and an idea occurred to him.

Mr Selkirk was still out on the lawn, though he had moved a few feet to the left. Nico went over to the piano stool. The padded seat, as is usual, doubled as a hinged lid, the space within the stool being designed to hold sheet music. Sheet music there was—Bach's '48', a Beethoven sonata or two, songs from the shows—but it lay at the bottom of the pile. The top half was constituted by printed or handwritten papers. Nico drew these out and began rifling through them: drafts of letters, rough notes on various subjects (Nietzsche, vitrification, a bit of a family tree), and finally, yes here it was, he knew the old man wouldn't destroy such a thing, couldn't bring himself to, *you never knew what you might need*. He removed it, closed the lid of the stool and returned to the desk by the window where he compared the document in his hand with its successor. Almost identical. But almost is not enough.

Mr Selkirk was moving. He walked a few paces, stopped, walked a few more paces, then without warning turned 90° and looked up directly at the study window, shading his eyes from the sun. Nico stepped back, not too swiftly. He knelt down on the floor and from his kneeling position gathered up all the documents on the desk bar two, depositing them in the open drawers more or less where he thought he had found them. Having closed the drawers he crawled on all fours to the door of the study, grasping a sheaf of papers; once clear of the window he got to his feet and dusted the knees of his trousers. He unbuttoned his shirt, stuffed the papers inside, re-buttoned his shirt and after a quick visual check of the room exited, closing the door behind him.

*

'Bonne nuit.'

'Bonne nuit, madame.'

From her station in the doorway of *Les Pêcheurs* Maia watched Béatrice set off down the road, a moonlit knapsacked figure keeping close to the grassy verge. Soon the figure was blending into the shadows, reappearing only when it passed underneath one of the sparsely planted lampposts, each time fainter and smaller. The stars were out, the air was fresh and night-scented. In the darkness not far off a horse whinnied. Maia breathed in deeply and thought about Johnny.

On the evening when they'd first opened the doors of *Les Pêcheurs* to the public they had come out together to stand just here, savouring the night and their sense of accomplishment, the last customer departed and money in the till. Not a huge amount, but a start. Johnny's elation made him even more talkative than usual. 'You can tell already which ones are going to be the regulars, that gangly painter and decorator for one, he must have put away a bottle of wine, we'll need to start thinking what food to serve, pops, the kitchen might need refurbishing, did you see that old couple in the corner who brought their own dominoes? ...' He was over the moon, his own master at last, running his own business (actually they'd both put money into the venture), and to cap it all living in a French village with horses in the next field. What could be better? Maia smiled at his happiness as at the excitement of a schoolboy on the first day of the summer holidays.

Johnny's happiness was infectious but Fournhac itself must get much of the credit. All these years later she could still taste the romance of her situation, at least sometimes, at least on nights like this. Sometimes it occurred to her she was better off this way, that if Johnny ever did see fit to return he would upset everything, steal her equilibrium as he had done once before and make her his slave. Or he might appear before her hunched and toothless, his last penny gone and whining to be taken back in his old age, no longer adorable but merely pathetic. In her memory he was always lithe and energetic with sparkling eyes, but in reality he must now be dim-eyed, arthritic, possibly senile...like Julius.

Like Julius. Disintegrating Julius. That was real, that was a present responsibility. It was something she had been unprepared for. In fact she'd bungled her reaction to it, saying too much or too little, even shedding tears in front of him. Some comfort! Still, they had talked, they had communed, and they could do so again. She would manage it better a second time. When he left this morning nothing definite had been said about meeting up but he was around for another week and seemed to have no other commitments. I will phone him, she decided. I will suggest visiting him in Uzès. I need to be proactive about this.

It was 11 p.m. She went back indoors and found her phone behind the bar. But wasn't it too late to call him? If he was asleep it would be a bad thing to wake him up—tomorrow morning would surely do. She held the phone in her hand and as she vacillated and pondered its blank screen the contraption came suddenly to life, the ring tone scattering the silence and the screen lighting up. The number displayed was Julius's.

'Hello, Maia? It's Julius. Sorry to be ringing you so late.'

'That's okay.'

'Are you around tomorrow? I'd like to come and see you again if you are. If you'd like that.' He sounded excited, a little breathless, the words running into each other.

'Of course I'd like that,' said Maia, settling herself on a bar stool. 'I was actually just about to ring you. You seem to be psychic.'

'You mean psycho.'

'Oh Julius . . .'

'That's great. Would it be okay if I brought a couple of people along for you to meet? One of them's trying to cajole me into agreeing to give a lecture for an institute his uncle runs. I'd like your opinion, Maia, you're such a wise person and I can't decide whether the institute in question is bona fide.'

'Bona fide?'

'Intellectually and morally respectable. But the thing is he's a very pleasant young man and his girlfriend is charming. Very simpatico, I mean simpatica, and bright as a button. We've just been having dinner together, the three of us. Talked about all sorts of things, politics, the environment, God, Australia...'

'The wine flowed, I take it?'

'May have done.'

'Do bring them along, Julius, they sound lovely. Are they French?'

'No, he's half-American and she's Australian. Travis and Kelly, sounds like a comedy duo, doesn't it.'

'What sort of time?'

'Mid-afternoon?'

'Fine. If I'm not at the pub I'll be up at the barn, or on my way to or from it.'

'I say Maia, do you think you'd like to do a painting of the girl? I told her you were a real artist. She's very striking and her quasi-father-in-law is a millionaire.'

Maia laughed. 'We can talk about that tomorrow. I'm so glad we can... I do look forward to seeing you again, Julius—it'll be...'

'I'm feeling a bit better today,' he said. It sounded like an apology.

Next day brought a breath of autumn, the sky overcast and the temperature a few degrees lower. In the morning the pub's ancient central heating had banged and groaned into action. Maia put on thick socks and a jumper. At lunchtime some of the customers at *Les Pêcheurs* turned up in coats. Brian Decker wore a scarf in the colours of what had been his local cricket team when he still lived in England in what he called his previous life. Perching on his usual bar stool he asked for a gin and tonic and said, 'Nippy out there.' His scarf sat neatly folded beside him on the counter. 'Wouldn't be surprised if it rained.'

'The farmers will be pleased,' said Maia. She dropped a lemon slice into the glass and took Brian's money.

'Ice and slice, sure signs of vice.' He raised the glass to his lips. 'By the way, how's that friend of yours doing, the visiting Englishman? Tall chap.'

'He returned to Uzès, but he'll be back later today. You were right about them grounding planes.'

'Yes, and Paris is in turmoil—you've heard the latest news, I suppose? The demonstrations have turned nasty, at least one policeman killed. They're talking about imposing a curfew. Bloody environmentalists. The authorities should start using rubber bullets, that's my humble opinion.'

'Some of the protests are justified, don't you think?'

'Like which?'

'That virology centre over near Valliguières surely ought to be stopped. Cutting down forests so they can experiment with viruses...'

'I don't much like it myself, but you can't go breaking the law and killing policemen. If people want to stop something they should use their vote. Ballot boxes before bombs.'

'What if there's no party that represents your views?'

'Then you should jolly well start one.'

'Easier said than done,' murmured George, who had been standing behind Brian for some time. Brian twitched his shoulders: 'There's that voice again. I think it's following me around.'

At 2.30 Maia drove the van up the hill, past the boulangerie, past the memorial garden, to park it where the road levelled out, close into the kerb and within sight of M. Bouvet's barn. Getting out of the van she felt two or three spots of rain on her skin. The footbridge over the brook wasn't yet wet, which was good. As she crossed it she saw that the barn door was open. Maia frowned; she distinctly remembered closing it yesterday evening. Could it have blown open in the wind? That seemed unlikely. Perhaps M. Bouvet was accustomed to coming into the barn to check up on things—it was his barn. Or someone might have turned up to look at, or take another look at, the pictures, though it would strike her as unusual for a local to go in pursuit of cultural stimulation before evening.

Maia entered and found the barn empty. She examined the requests book to see if someone had registered an interest in anything since yesterday; there was nothing new. Dropping the blue exercise book back on the table she walked over to the standard lamp, which had given out the day before, and was in the process of removing the bulb when her peripheral vision alerted her to something out of place, something off-key. Even before she turned her head she knew what she would see, knew that Johnny's charcoal feet were once again emerging from a tangle of lines to kick the air.

Maia stood still, the dead light bulb inches from her face. A gentle murmur of rain reached her through the open door. She pocketed the bulb and approached Johnny's upside-down portrait, scanning its chaotic shapes as if it were the work of another artist. It's like an inverted Ascension, she thought. One of those naïve depictions of Christ's feet protruding from a cloud, but the other way up. The Descent. The Descent of Johnny Byrne, headlong and earthward bound, a fallen angel. She examined the picture and its surroundings, seeking clues, what sort of clues she herself didn't know. The Bouvet children wouldn't play such a joke twice; this was some kind of message, a move in an obscure game. Something to be interpreted.

Her eyes slid down the barn wall and rested on a yellow object lying on the ground. There wasn't much light to see by—the day was overcast and the standard lamp wasn't working. But she recognised what it was. Bending over, Maia picked up the sunflower and brought it close to her face. A faint odour of summer came from it.

*

When they came in out of the rain, into the earthy woody atmosphere of the barn, having got out of the car and trooped across the little footbridge with its wobbly handrail, Kelly saw a woman with grey frizzy hair near the other end of the barn holding a flower. She was wearing an oilskin jacket and although the light was dim Kelly was pretty sure she was crying, or at any rate shaking, trembling. That is Maia, she thought, Maia the artist.

'Here we are, bringing the weather with us,' Julius called out. He was advancing towards the woman with one arm outstretched. 'They've seen the pub. I said you'd be up here in your salon.'

The woman wiped her face and managed a blanched sort of smile. She came to meet him and they embraced under the central light bulb. Kelly thought of mistletoe.

Travis was hunting for the light switch. 'Dark in here,' he said, finding it. A spotlight fell on the two figures as on a cabaret act and they separated, holding hands and looking into one another's faces. Travis hovered near the light switch wondering if he shouldn't restore them to semi-privacy, decided against it.

'Julius,' said the woman.

But Julius was already moving, pulling her with him. 'Come and meet Travis and Kelly—Travis and Kelly, meet my bestest and oldest friend Maia Byrne, whose paintings you see all around you. There's even one of me—look, behind you Travis, don't you think the cravat affected? I was young and foolish. Never wear a cravat.'

They had driven up from Uzès, Kelly in the front listening to Julius's talk, Travis behind her leaning forwards in his seat. (She could smell the coffee on his breath.) Julius chattered all the way from Uzès to Fournhac, though chatter wasn't really the word for it, it was more like a cross between someone giving a lecture and sleep-talking. At dinner the previous evening he had been similarly lively but more interactive. Perhaps the wine had helped. She liked him, she liked his talk, but there was something wrong with him and she was afraid that Travis's 'assignment' was probably doomed, if that mattered at all in the scheme of things. Travis had happily acquiesced to the idea of a day trip to Fournhac since he thought it showed the professor was yielding, and Kelly didn't mind the change of scene. Shame about the weather.

Travis was having the paintings explained to him. Maia Byrne spoke with soft precision. She had a broad forehead underneath the mass of hair and her brown eyes were like pools. Every now and then she would gesture at the canvases with a hand which still held onto the flower, a sunflower Kelly now saw. Julius was looking over Maia's shoulder.

'What a shock it must have been. You're living an ordinary humdrum newly-married sort of life when a messenger of God appears and you find out that you're to be at the centre of the most extraordinary events of human history.'

Travis nodded. 'Uh-huh. I see what you mean.'

'And you have no choice in the matter,' Maia went on. 'But some things can only come to you if you don't choose them. Life itself, for instance.'

'I love all that blue,' said Julius. 'Blue, blue, blue.' He waved a hand.

Through the door of the barn came the smell of rain on earth, clean and fresh. The central light bulb flickered, once, twice. We are four characters in a group portrait, thought Kelly, two women and two men. Or six if you include Mary and the angel.

'But you didn't come here to view an exhibition,' Maia said. 'Tell me about yourselves. You're staying in Uzès, aren't you? Are you on holiday?'

As before, Travis glanced enquiringly at Julius and as before, Julius remained impassive. 'Well,' began Travis, 'my uncle, Harry Selkirk, has set up a new institute called the Optimex Foundation, devoted to—to bettering the world, I guess. He'd like Professor Durward to give the inaugural lecture. He's a great admirer of Professor Durward's work.'

'*Pandora's Mirror?*'

'Yes. And so he sent me to talk to Professor Durward about it—I'm his PA. And we met in Uzès yesterday, and had dinner, and now today... Professor Durward thought it would be nice—let's go to Fournhac, he said...'

'It's good to meet you,' said Maia, 'I'm glad Julius brought you.' Turning to Kelly: 'Julius thinks I ought to paint you, Kelly, I can see why. You're beautiful. But you've been very quiet. I'm afraid we've all been talking too much.'

'That's okay, I often don't say a lot,' replied Kelly. Travis made a noise between coughing and choking. Kelly smiled at Maia and said, 'I like the sunflower. Are you going to paint it?'

Maia looked down at the flower in her hand and was about to say something when Julius spoke, addressing them: 'The proclaimed aim of the Optimex Foundation is to lead us to a future without disease and poverty, with no war and plenty for all.'

He was standing with his hands in his pockets, looking a few inches above their heads. Shoulders pushed back, glasses perched on a beaky nose. In front of him the ghost of a lectern.

'It is a noble ideal. What are we here for except to make the world a better place? Of course when we arrive at that earthly paradise there'll be a question what to do with ourselves now all the problems have been solved. No point in hanging onto that noble ideal, it will have served its purpose, we can throw it away like a used condom. No point in looking into the future, making prognostications, worrying about tomorrow. The lilies of the field toil not, neither do they spin. We are to be like lilies.'

'I think we are meant to love one another,' said Maia. 'Lilies don't love.'

'Mr Selkirk...' started Travis.

'Mr Selkirk must be a remarkable man,' interrupted Julius, beginning to pace up and down. 'As well as rich he is, I believe, elderly, and yet his love for his fellow human beings enables him to see beyond his own annihilation to a world in whose joys and sufferings he will have no part. And yet I wonder if his conception of that world has any real substance. It is to be a world without disease, without warfare, lacking this and lacking that and lacking the other. A negatively defined world. Mr Selkirk, it strikes me, is an apophatic theologian, would you not agree, Mr Beggs?'

Travis merely blinked.

'The God of his theology, I presume, is something like Progress, or General Utility. Many sacrifices have already been made to this God, its nostrils are filled with the incense of burnt offerings, the smell of human flesh, particulates rising in clouds from the camp incinerators. It is a hungry God. But we can know nothing of it until we meet it face to face, that is the apophatic message. We can know nothing, except negatives, about the world where Progress is leading us, and among all the *withouts* of that world the one of which I confess I am afraid, the one that sends a chill to my soul, is *without a history*. When we have spent so long gazing into the future, the always retreating and non-existent future, isn't it possible that we'll finally cease to be able to turn our heads and look behind us, where our own past, our own selves, are to be found? We will have lost our selves. Nothing matters that's only been around for thirty seconds, that's obvious, that's why Russell's thought experiment is so worrying, why Korsakoff syndrome sounds like hell on earth, but to *invite* amnesia, to court it, to volunteer for it...'

'But why should improving the human condition result in all that stuff?' Travis was roused at last. Julius's tirade seemed to him superstition, obscurantism. Was this the real message of *Pandora's Mirror*? That vaccines and peace-keeping forces will turn us all into zombies? 'For one thing,' he went on, 'in a world in which wealth is more evenly distributed more people can go to college to study history.'

'But will they? Why study history when they can study maths or medicine? They've been told that education is either a means to personal affluence or preparation for insertion into the great social machine, or both. Economist-priests tell them that rational action aims at maximizing utility—that the thirst for knowledge, along with loyalty and gratitude and honour, has only instrumental value. Studying history will be of use to the extent that it supplies evidence for the proposition that doing X will get you more goodies than doing Y. An aid to political decision-making.'

'Is that valueless?'

'No, it's not valueless.' Julius stopped his pacing. 'And memories of first love can provide sound evidential support for middle-aged life-choices. But why do we keep mementoes of those we've loved? Why do we visit their graves? Are we *stupid*?'

His voice rose on the last word; Maia made a move towards him, an appeasing hand half-raised. She wants to protect him, thought Kelly.

'No, sir, of course not.' Travis was backing off, he was recalling his assignment. 'You're absolutely right. But shouldn't we then reform the schools and universities? That would make a really interesting theme for a lecture: the importance of the humanities in an age of science. I think Mr Selkirk would appreciate that idea, sir.'

Julius looked tired. He went over to a chair by the wall and sat down. Kelly said: 'You should talk about whatever you want to. In your lecture. It's bound to be interesting.' She turned to Maia. 'Don't you think so?'

'Of course,' said Maia. 'Of course any lecture by Julius Durward will be interesting. And important.'

Julius rubbed his hair, took off his glasses, put them back on. 'So do you think I should accept the invitation? Maia?'

'Yes, Julius. Accept the invitation. Accept it.'

*

As a new member of the department Julius had to give a public lecture at the end of his second semester. In practice 'public' meant the rest of the university, so he was expecting an audience of staff and students divided 50-50 between historians and non-historians. He chose for a title 'Origins and outcomes of the French wars of religion'. Americans appeared to be still interested in religion, unlike their cynical European cousins, and war was always interesting to everybody. In front of an audience of nearly two hundred people he stood behind a lectern, hands sweaty with nerves, talking into a microphone about the trail of blood which led from the Albigensian Crusade to the St Bartholomew's Day Massacre. Why France and not England? Why does the camel have a hump?

In the front row sat a slim dark girl taking notes. When she wasn't taking notes she was looking straight at him, eyes interrogative and humorous. Afterwards at the drinks reception she introduced herself.

'Hi, I'm Toni Ferrari. I loved your talk. That Simon de Montford guy sounds like a psychopath.'

'It was a crueller age. And what do you do?'

'I'm a doctoral student. English literature.'

They talked for half an hour about George Eliot. In the evening he walked her back to her apartment.

*

'It'll be great,' said Kelly. 'I'll definitely be there. Where's it going to happen, Trav?'

'That's really up to the professor,' Travis replied. 'It could be in the UK, or in the States... or even here, I guess. I mean, maybe Paris.'

Julius was staring into space, hands on knees, fingers of the right hand tapping rhythmically. Outside the rain had stopped.

'Sir?...'

'Let me think,' barked Julius.

Maia walked off in the direction of a lamp standing in a corner of the barn. On the way she paused by a window and placed the sunflower on the sill. Then she produced two light bulbs, one from each jacket pocket, examined them, and returned the left-hand one. Her movements were studied and graceful; Kelly watched her with pleasure as she might watch a dancer. The ceremony continued. Maia was by the standard lamp now. Crouching a little, she fed the light bulb under the shade to an unseen lamp holder, then stood up straight.

Julius got to his feet. 'Mr Beggs,' he said. 'You can tell Mr Selkirk that I am happy to accept his invitation.'

There was a click and the barn brightened. Kelly felt like clapping.

'But at the moment I cannot vouchsafe him a title.'

Travis had bounded forward. 'Professor Durward, I'm so pleased, thank you so much—this is wonderful. On behalf of the Optimex Foundation may I...'

'Yes, yes,' muttered Julius, going back to his chair. 'Wait till you get it.'

'Celebratory drinks will be served at *Les Pêcheurs*,' announced Maia with a smile.

Not doomed after all, thought Kelly.

*

Back in his room, Nico unbuttoned his shirt and extracted the documents. He deposited them on the seat of a wingback armchair, mouldy but comfortable. The Last and the Last-but-one Will and Testament of Harry D Selkirk. The last shall be first and the first shall be last says the Good Book. Nico had always been a religious man, his parents had brought him up to be a good Catholic, scriptural texts were familiar to him. Vengeance is mine saith the Lord was another one. But this wasn't vengeance. It was justice.

He felt in the pocket of a dressing gown hanging on the back of the door and produced a pack of cigarettes. Mr Selkirk prohibited smoking on the premises but he rarely ascended the stairs to Nico's room, a garret at the back of the house with a dormer window through which only the sky was visible. This window Nico now opened. A blackbird's singing accompanied him as he lit up. The documents stared back at him from the chair.

Ten years of service and this is my reward. *Hijo de puta.*

The blackbird paused and Nico strained his ears; in the far distance another blackbird was singing, replying to the first, conversing with it. The birds of the air have no need of wills and testaments, employment contracts, court summonses, none of these things. They speak their heart. With words and with language the human being lies and robs, but an animal speaks its heart.

Hijo de puta.

An old writing bureau stood against a wall and from one of its drawers Nico extracted a fountain pen and a blotter. A cigarette hung from the corner of his mouth, smoke curling upwards. Kneeling, he divided the pile of papers into two and placed the halves side by side on the floor: on the right hand the older document, on the left the impostor, the usurper. He picked up the right hand sheaf of papers and pulled out the last page, at the bottom of which was Mr Selkirk's dated signature. Nico removed the lid of the fountain pen. By changing a 1 into a 4 and a 7 into a 9 he brought the date forward by approximately two and a half years. Having thus pre-empted the meddlings of any attorney who might happen to have a copy of the later Will, he now turned his attention to that document. Then shall he say also unto them on the left hand, Depart from me, ye cursed, into everlasting fire, Matthew 25:41.

When Mr Selkirk originally moved into The Vines he installed central heating. Fireplaces were messy and labour-intensive, a thing of the past. Most of the chimneys in the house had been blocked up. An exception was Nico's room: it didn't seem worthwhile putting a radiator up in that cubbyhole, as Doreen used to call it, so Mr Selkirk left it as it was, with a functioning fireplace and an old electric heater which Nico was encouraged not to make too much use of and which in any case was temperamental in its workings. By contrast the fireplace was remarkably efficient.

Tshi went the cigarette lighter and the corner of the top page caught, the flame spreading and growing. Words were eaten up, legal provisions were made void. Nico held the paper until the last moment and dropped the wispy blackened remnant into the fireplace. Again the lighter went *tshi* and a second page was devoured. Gradually the pile shrank. Half way through Nico lit another cigarette. A poker leant on the wall to the side of the hearth and with this he prodded and broke up the filaments of paper. He continued with his job until sitting on the floor in front of him was the true, the only Will of Harry D Selkirk while in the grate beside him was a heap of anonymous ashes and a single burning page from which rose a thread of smoke, the last expiring breath of a Judas-snake.

A quarter of a mile away Mr Selkirk was seated on the garden bench which was the midpoint of his regular afternoon constitutional. The bench afforded him a fine view of the house and he was enjoying that view and the sense of proprietorship which it still faintly evoked. From one of the chimneys a trickle of smoke emerged. Selkirk squinted; it was the chimney to Nico's room. Could he be lighting a fire in August? No, it was September now—even so, warm enough. The smoke had stopped; perhaps it had been an illusion, he was having his monthly eye test in a few days, might mention it to the optician. He couldn't remember when he'd last been up to that room. Years ago. There was a dormer window and a sofa, unless he'd got rid of the sofa; it was on that sofa that he and Doreen had made love when she'd suggested they fuck in every room in the house, starting from the top—a kind of ritual anointing of the marital home. He chuckled at the recollection. Start in the garret, end up in the cellar. Not all within twenty-four hours of course, he might have been a stud in his thirties but The Vines was a big place. Doing it in the kitchen had been best, he'd taken her on the kitchen table, Doreen with her legs up on his shoulders wailing like a banshee. But the sofa in the garret had been good. If he wasn't mistaken they'd lit candles.

What a contrast with the later time, the time when Doreen retreated into herself, drifting round the house with that empty face. Damn foetus did that to her, maybe they'd conceived it in their ritual fucking-spree, the chronology eluded him now, but what a damn hellish thing to happen to her, to his dear lovely Doreen, she didn't deserve it, she didn't deserve that damn miscarriage. Sure, the SSRIs perked her up but it was never the same again. Never.

He looked over at the house and saw a figure moving around in his study, Nico doing some dusting and cleaning. What a godsend Nico was. Selkirk consulted his watch. Time to go in, time to ring his nephew. Find out what was happening in France, if anything.

*

They'd had dinner in a little restaurant off the Place aux Herbes. Strolling back to the hotel arm in arm they detoured down side streets and peered through railings. The rain clouds had sailed on and it was a clear night, though the wind hadn't died; a gust would meet them as they turned a corner and Kelly would cry out, delighted. In the shadow of the duchy Travis pulled her to him and kissed her hard. He was triumphant.

'Look at the moon, Trav. It's gibbous.'

'It's what?'

'Gibbous. And the terminator is as clear as anything.'

'You're pulling my leg. Or showing off. Come on, let's get back to the hotel.'

He started moving but she stayed where she was, gazing up. A cat darted across the Place du Duché and disappeared into the shadows. There were no other people.

'It's beautiful here, isn't it, Trav. Nights more beautiful than our days…'

'You Romantic. Come here, Romantic.' He held out his hand.

Julius had left them a few hours ago saying he wanted an early night. On the journey back from Fournhac he'd been quiet and withdrawn; Travis had done most of the talking, with Kelly contributing a joke about a three-legged pig. They'd agreed to all meet up again in a couple of days. Julius needed to be reminded that Philippe the crazy anarchist would be turning up, wanting a lift to somewhere or other—also that he'd promised him a pamphlet. Privately Travis hoped that the pamphlet, if it ever got written, wouldn't receive much publicity: that would detract from the *coup* of the inaugural lecture. Moreover he doubted whether his uncle would find views like those of Philippe Arentz congenial, indeed the virology institute was just the sort of thing he'd take as an embodiment of enlightened progress. Yes, Durward was right, Progress was Uncle Harry's god. And did the professor have a better one?

'That's the last of it,' said Kelly. They were back in their hotel room. She tapped a few final granules onto the mirror. 'We'll have to start on the other earring soon.'

Travis lolled on the floor beside her watching what she was doing. 'Do you ever think about the drug barons, all that killing and torture and stuff?'

Kelly began cutting the coke. 'Yes, Trav, I do. And when I'm eating bacon I quite often think of the blood flowing in the slaughterhouses. The difference is that coke's illegal. If you legalized it the barons would disappear and the killing would stop. Bacon's already legal, it's going to be hard to make it any less fatal for pigs.'

'Good point.'

'I'm full of good points.'

'But pigs aren't people.'

'Though some people are pigs.' She snorted a line.

'Okay, you've convinced me,' he said, taking the rolled-up note.

Kelly stood up and stretched. 'See y'all soon.' Barefooted she headed for the bathroom.

'We landed him, didn't we,' Travis called out a moment later. 'Finally hooked him … He was *this* big.'

(Arms stretched out to either side.) 'Travis Beggs goes deep sea fishing and, with the help of his lovely assistant, catches an intellectual celebrity, to be served up in the near future with—with a hollandaise sauce, plus chips, at a magnificent feast to be hosted by the world-famous Optimex...'

His phone was ringing. He reached for it under the table. It was Uncle Harry.

'How's it going, Travis? Any news about your flight?'

'My flight? Ah ... No, sir, no news about that, but I have some great news about the professor, we had a long talk and discussed the idea of the inaugural lecture at length—a really in-depth discussion, sir...' He licked a fingertip, touched some remaining grains of white powder, brought it to his tongue. Sharp, anaesthetizing.

'Well? Go on. What did he say?'

Travis grinned. Kelly had appeared in the doorway of the bathroom, naked. Her arms were crossed artfully across her breasts and she pouted a kiss at him.

'He said ... wow ... He said *yessirree*, gimme some of that.'

'He what?'

'Sorry, sir, I think the line is—' Tears of laughter, his whole body shaking. Travis coughed hard so as to get a hold of himself. 'That's ... Something happened with my throat there, sir. The fact is, Professor Durward has accepted the invitation.'

'He's accepted? You say he's accepted?'

'Yessirree. Yes, sir.'

'That's tremendous. Well done, Travis, I thought I could count on you. Have you talked about topics? A venue?'

'I'll be seeing him again the day after tomorrow and will make sure to get answers to those very questions. What shall I say about payment, sir? How's that going to be arranged?'

'Send me his bank details, I can transfer the sum immediately. That'll show him we're for real. Travis?'

'Yes, sir?' He held up his foot. Kelly was removing his left shoe.

'I may as well tell you now—I've written my will. You're the main beneficiary.'

And the right shoe.

'Of course I don't mean to die anytime soon, I've got a few more years left in me, my doctor seems to think so anyway.'

Socks. Shirt buttons.

'But blood is thicker than water, you're my half-sister's son—and as well as all that you're a capable, responsible young man, someone with intelligence and ambition, someone who's ready to carve out a place for himself in the world. It's the Selkirk blood, Travis. Your father was a good man, he was very good to Deborah...'

Belt, trousers, boxer shorts.

'...the whole place, you can live in it or sell it, that'll be up to you...'

View of the top of Kelly's head. Warm thunder spreading through his body.

'... I hope you're pleased. I've tried to do the right thing by you, Travis. Travis, are you still there?'

'Sir ... I'm more grateful ... more grateful than I can say.'

Kelly whispering.

'What?'

'What?'

'Hang up, Trav.'

'I have to go now, sir. I think the professor's trying to ring me.'

'Okay, Travis. You better talk to him.'

VIII

A JUDDERY FIGURE WEARING A balaclava reached back and with the deliberate grace of an athlete flung his arm forward. A few feet in front of the line of uniforms and shields the tarmac erupted in a burst of flame. Smoke drifted across the scene, illuminated here and there by the fires of burning cars or buildings. The camera wheeled round and a ragtag crowd came into view, youths lobbing missiles, running, standing, yelling silently between cupped hands. Near the bottom of the screen a ribbon of subtitles moved sedately from right to left.

Julius pressed the volume on his remote control and distant sounds of battle emerged from the flat screen TV, coming nearer as he pressed again, dying when he muted them. By his elbow stood a bottle of Peroni beer from the mini fridge.

Those could be Philippe's students. You want anarchy? Here it is. Paris in flames. Like the good old days, the days of '68, and before that 1830 and before that 1789. Let's hope the Rebex gang don't start guillotining people. On the screen a policeman with blood streaming down his face staggers off stage left.

But it's peace they want: a cessation of hostilities. No more warring against Mother Nature, no more killing and raping of the environment. Let the trees grow and the birds sing and the coal lie sleeping in the earth. If anything is to be destroyed it's the greed in men's hearts. The temple of Mammon is to be razed, brick by brick it is to be dismantled, the grabbing and the looting are to stop once and for all.

Philippe, mon vieux! I love you and I love your vision. To return to Paradise: what better aim? Here's to you and here's to your Paradise.

He took a swig of the Peroni and wiped his mouth with the back of his hand.

But what is Paradise, they ask? What is it and where is it? Are we to build it from scratch? Is it to be a gleaming city, a Dubai-for-all, megalopolitan playground? Baubles and geegaws. Seek rather the hermit's cell, the rye bread and the brackish water. Or a candle stuck in the neck of a wine bottle and a plate of croissants. Maia sits opposite, she is smiling through her tears. Words come out of my mouth, the story I tell is intricate and technical. A human brain contains approximately ninety billion neurons and in the fine mesh constituted by the myriad connections between them rents may appear, small tears in the fabric of one's mind, odd pages missing from random books on the shelves of a well-stocked library. 'Once upon a time there lived an old with his suddenly the horse bolted whispered the fairy dead.'

But modern science has invented a cure, or if not a cure a palliative, or if not a palliative a spade to dig a hole with, and into the hole goes . . . Now Maia has placed her hand upon mine. She smiles through her tears and says *He is alive, he is not dead.* Our fingers intertwine. I do not understand her.

A policeman wearing a visor is laying into a youth on the ground with his truncheon. The scene cuts back to the studio where a grave-faced anchor man mouths information and statistics.

The name of the cure is Alethex. *Aletheia*: Greek for truth, from *a-* meaning not and *lethe* meaning forgetfulness. I am a seeker after truth. With the help of my little yellow pills I will banish forgetfulness, destroy oblivion and reclaim my inheritance.

The clock on the wall said 22:31. One more dose before bedtime. He filled a glass with water in the bathroom and took it to his bedside table. The book of Yeats poetry was still there, scarcely touched since his arrival. 'Things fall apart; the centre cannot hold.' Bugger that. Where are my pills? Not in the drawer—somewhere else then. He looked around the room. Mayhem had returned to the flat screen, not Paris this time but some other city, Nantes perhaps or Lyon. The rioting was spreading, good luck to them, try not to kill too many policemen, chaps.

He spotted the blue packet sitting on an arm of the sofa. Must have put it there after taking his last dose, whenever that was. Counting the remaining pills he found he had about twelve days' supply. He'd need to get a repeat prescription on his return, whenever that would be. Whenever, whenever: quoth the Raven 'Whenever'. A prettier song than 'Nevermore'. He popped a pill, drank some water, tilted back his head and swallowed.

Earlier or later he sat in the hotel lobby eating peanuts and salami, a glass of red wine to keep him company. The young man with the ponytail was chatting with some other guests, a middle-aged couple, he fat she thin, fluent French-speakers, maybe they *were* French. Were they coming or going? Neither, it would seem. As he watched them he recalled another couple appearing through the hotel doors, young and good-looking, coming into the lobby and making a beeline for him, he wearing a jacket and tie she in a white summery number. They'd all gone off to look at the cathedral and the Racine pavilion, the boy had talked to his boss on the phone, the girl had asked him about Henri de Crussol. Later they'd bumped into Philippe in the Place aux Herbes.

Julius, you do remember things.

Thank you, Maia.

And if the things get a bit muddled up, at any rate you still remember them.

That's true, Maia.

Maybe some of the things you remember didn't happen, but that just adds to life's riches, don't you think? Better too much than too little.

Absolutely.

He nibbled at the salami, very perfect pabulum, the Sicilians make it out of donkeys' meat. Through the hotel doors came a middle-aged couple, he fat she thin.

The ponytailed youth engaged them in conversation. The boy, the other one, was hoping to inveigle him into giving a lecture to his uncle's outfit, an institute devoted to improving the world. Well, it needed to improve. But what would he lecture on? If he were unscrupulous he could plagiarise his former self, cut and paste ideas out of *Pandora's Mirror*, reheat an old soup. Wasn't that what they wanted in any case? More of the same? 'Dear Mr Rachmaninov, won't you just play that lovely C# minor prelude again?' *Nyet* mutters Sergei but Sergei's an old miseryguts, Julius is more amenable; 'Shall I give you that old Pandora jazz, sir, the one you liked so much the first time? You can sing along at the chorus, Mr Selkirk, sir.' Crumbly Mr Selkirk nods approval and in a moment he's raising his cracked voice to the strains of 'I Did it My Way'. Stuck on a desert island of self-made wealth he dreams of Utopia and the ship that'll carry him there, the SS Optimex. His nephew stands at the helm, bare-breasted Kelly is the figurehead with flowing golden hair who scans the horizon with azure eyes. Maia sits on deck at her easel and paints her.

On the TV screen the gyrating blue light of an ambulance speeds past. The camera follows it, as do the phones of filming pedestrians—rioters? Tourists? One of them's standing near the camera; the ambulance is duplicated in miniature, there are two of it taking two loads of damaged humanity to two invisible hospitals. Julius sees it pulling up near the hospital entrance where a couple of paramedics help somebody out. They put him in a wheelchair and Julius follows them through the swing doors into a busy concourse, along a corridor to a lift, they ride the lift up to the fourth floor, the two paramedics chatting of trivial things while the boy in the wheelchair sits quite still, his pale face saying nothing. Only when someone comes into the lift whose knee carelessly jolts the frame of the wheelchair does a tremor of pain disturb the still surface, red eyes narrowing. Anger catches at Julius's throat but now the lift doors are opening and they are trooping out, down the empty corridor, turn right at the bottom, follow signs for Haematology.

He got another Peroni from the mini fridge. As he closed the fridge door his attention was caught by ink marks on his wrist. It was writing: *Philippe Sunday.* He remembered—the two of them were going to drive into the woods to pay a clandestine visit to a projected building site. Languedoc's answer to Porton Down. The happy band of pioneers would be meeting them, Andy the computer whizzkid, duffle-coated Raoul, Eva. Eva who was sleeping with Philippe, Eva who wanted to clog up the courts and the prisons. And someone called Max. Sunday morning—whenever that was. Perhaps it had already happened? No, he couldn't forget so much so quickly. Not yet. Usefully, the clock on the wall displayed the syllable SAM, for Samedi. 'My God, Holmes, you're a genius.' Tomorrow, then. Into the woods on the trail of CIRI. And a pamphlet or news article or blog to be written, an exposé of French folly by a disinterested but interested outsider, the renowned British author of a puzzlingly multifaceted treatise admired by, among others, Harry D Selkirk. Yes, the American philanthropist, rich as Croesus and probably a fool, has taken *Pandora's Mirror* to his heart and desires the imprimatur of its distinguished creator, whose market value he relies on to give his hare-brained venture a kick start. But what will Croesus-Crusoe think when he reads about the author's denunciation of a research centre whose proclaimed aim is to arm mankind against the threats posed by viral pandemics? Will Crusoe-Croesus not wonder if he's been backing the wrong horse? For that matter, will Comrade Arentz not baulk at his old friend's endorsement of a utilitarian-capitalist millenarian fantasy? A man cannot serve two masters. They both want me to proclaim their visions, that's the problem. But I'm not even looking in the same direction as them. I'm looking to Arcadia, I'm looking to the Elysian Fields, where smiling shades converse with one another and a ghostly cat called Caleb miaows silently by the Aga. Three ghosts on bicycles ride up an Oxfordshire hill, halt on the crest to admire the view. Johnny points to a distant huddle of houses and says 'Rose and Crown'.

'Will it still be open?' asks Maia.

'Should be—it's not yet two. Might as well try. What do you think, Jules?'

Julius nods. 'I'm game.'

The trio descend the hill between trees and hedgerows into the sunlit valley. The pub is still open when they arrive hot and thirsty, and the place serves lunch. They lean their bikes against a wall, Johnny locking his to Maia's, Julius trusting to fate. Inside it's cool and dim, a low oak-beamed ceiling causes Julius to stoop, Maia is petting a shaggy dog while Johnny inspects the menu. The landlord stops talking to another customer and turns his attention to the newcomers: 'What can I get you?'

They sit outside in the garden, three plastic chairs drawn up to a filigree metal table. Some washing is hanging on a line strung between the pub wall and an apple tree: a sheet, two shirts, something pink and un-identifiable. Between the trees at the bottom of the gar-den they can see a river or stream, water flowing from left to right; the lazy sound of a chainsaw comes to them from half a mile away. The dog comes out of the pub and lays its head on Maia's knee. While they wait for their lunch they talk of this and that, Johnny nursing a Guin-ness, Maia a glass of white wine, Julius a pint of Hook Norton.

The interval before lunch. A place of peace: thoughts and sensations forever caught in amber. Happiness *sub specie aeterni.*

He sipped his wine and settled further down into the black leather armchair. Too comfortable, too encom-passing. I'm here to stay, guys, you'll have to hoist me out with a winch. Might as well hunker down since the planes aren't flying and Nîmes will probably be next to burn, could get hit by a Molotov cocktail if I so much as try to return my hire car. Wonder if they'll succeed. Or do any good at all. *Can* climate change be stopped? *Will* the authorities ever do anything? Perhaps it is sufficient to be a witness to the truth. Letting off steam also has its attractions. Philippe is a very articulate man, his arguments and his rhetoric combine to intoxicate, but his motivation is possibly suspect. He is perhaps not trustworthy. Nevertheless I love him.

The hotel doors open and a middle-aged couple walk in, he fat she thin. The youth with the ponytail addresses them, smiling, 'Bon soir m'sieur, madame.'

Where did Johnny go? Did he feel homesick? Did he succumb to a yearning for the Atlantic wind, for the gentle rain upon the emerald hills? 'I will arise and go now, and go to Innisfree.' So maybe he's living alone in a bee-loud glade on the west coast of Ireland, though it seems more likely he's formed a new ménage, lady's man that he always was and presumably still is. He might have met a pretty French girl and moved in with her twenty kilometres down the road. Leaving everything to Maia, of course—the pub, the work, the solitude and the memories. But she has her God and her God will look after her.

Johnny was a force of nature, you might say. Very energetic, very magnetic, a little bestial. He was aware of the effect he had on people, which could be either positive or negative, or both at the same time. Charisma, they call it. I imagine his mother spoilt him rotten. When he smiled or laughed it was very hard not to smile or laugh in sympathy, though he perhaps played the fool more than he needed to. He was generous, funny, could be sentimental on occasion. And was a complete narcissist.

Julius tapped rhythmically on his right knee with finger and thumb. He stared at the ceiling. The phone behind reception began to ring but there was no one there to answer it and after a while it stopped. Narcissists I have known. Johnny... Hugh, definitely... Philippe? *It takes one to know one, Durward.* Toni once said: 'I sometimes wonder if your love for Paul isn't really a form of self-love.' Does that make it bad? Anyway it depends what you mean. Toni probably meant 'You love Paul more than you love me.' So who's the narcissist?

What does it matter anyway? Why go on about it?

His own parents. Father a lawyer, mother a schoolteacher, he the apple of their eye. No siblings. Father worked hard, drank moderately, got Alzheimer's, ended up in a home. He was lucky to die before the Covid-19 pandemic when virus and government joined forces to cut a swathe through the elderly care home population. Mother a merry widow, passed away... recently, unless she's still alive? She can't be, she'd be a hundred or something, give or take a decade. Julia, née... that's the security question they used to ask you when you phoned them about your bank account or medical history: mother's maiden name? Before you can access this data, sir, we need you to tell us, come on you can remember, surname beginning with M, or is it R, Julia, Julia...

Funny to name the son after his mother.

The telephone at reception was ringing again. The chic receptionist answered it, 'Allo, Hotel Jaurès?' She inspected her painted nails, fingers splayed, turned them this way and that in the light.

Julius was in the lift, going up. Mother, Toni, Maia. The verb to love in three persons, first person, second person and third person. Though in reality Maia was the second person and Toni the third person. Your mother is always the first person, her love for you is first-personal, it is a form of self-love, does that make it bad? The Greeks had a taxonomy of love, philia (Maia), eros (Toni), storgē (Mother). Philautia is self-love. But there is much overlapping and blending. Toni was a friend as well as a lover, in Maia's philia there are warm whispers of eros, while storgē and philautia are intertwined: a parent's love is at once selfish and selfless. Mysterious and wonderful.

On the screen a man was talking to reporters, microphones were jostling in front of his face and cameras flashed. The subtitles flowed from right to left like water, like the river at the bottom of a pub garden. Julius felt he'd seen the face before somewhere. If I had been Albertine… It was one Daniel Leblanc, professeur, explaining the reasons (private and complicated) for his recent extended absence (disappearance in fact) and emphatically rejecting any suggestion that pressure of a political nature had been brought to bear on him in his capacity as etc. etc. He expressed the hope that irresponsible speculations by certain interested parties would now cease to be aired and that he could return to the exercise of his public and private duties free from the intrusions of a prurient press. The cameras flashed some more and Professor Leblanc was hustled away out of the picture. I'd have disparu too, thought Julius, no doubt about it. The game's not worth the candle, boyo, either Rebex will get you or the French secret service, bundle you into a van and take you somewhere they can coach you in what to say and what not to say. More carrot than stick, I'm sure, but that's not a great consolation when the carrot sticks in your throat at the thought of all those diggers and pile-drivers raping the ancient forests of the dukes of Uzès. And who allowed it? The family were not asked. No request was received, orally or in writing, my seneschal would have given me notice, he is a conscientious servant. My God! What trespass, what violation is now contemplated. Those lands have belonged to the House of Crussol for centuries and in those woods we have hunted at our leisure, the boar, the deer—flesh for great feasts, a very perfect pabulum, washed down with the blood-red wine of our vineyards. I will hie me thither, stand before the intruders with drawn sword. Ferro non auro. The king will hear my case.

Julius perched on the arm of the sofa drinking Peroni. On the wall clock 00.00 appeared and SAM became DIM. An ad for skin cream played out silently on the TV screen, smiling face, dabbing of cheeks.

And there she was, standing in front of the bathroom mirror rubbing the cool white moisturizer into her forehead and under her dark eyes. Toni in her silk pyjamas, Toni whose reflection smiled at him as he stood watching her. It was evening outside, the yellow blur of nearby lights wobbled in the frosted glass of the window. Julius leant against the wall, arms crossed on his bare chest.

'I'm almost certain,' she said. 'It's been six and a half weeks.'

'Since your last period?'

'Yes. And—I just feel it, you know?'

'A person can feel pregnant?'

She wiped away a smudge of skin cream with a tissue, threw it into the toilet.

'I'll get a test kit from Walgreens tomorrow. Julius,' she turned to him, 'aren't you excited? Isn't it exciting?'

'I'll have to get used to the idea of sharing you with someone else.' He hugged her, kissed her hair. 'Goes against the grain. But yes—darling, it's wonderful news. You're a star. Let's wait till you do the test, though.'

They went into the bedroom—Toni drew the curtains. There was a vase of freesias on the table. She removed a hairband and the black hair fell around her shoulders.

'What shall we call him?'

'Or her.'

'It's a boy, I'm sure of it.'

They lay down side by side on the bed looking into each other's eyes.

'I don't know. John? Richard?'

'Paul,' she said.

*

Julius had dozed off. In his hand he still held the Peroni bottle, nearly empty, and on the TV screen a football match was in progress, white shirts vs red shirts. Close-up of the referee: left hand pointing to the sky, right hand holding the whistle to his lips. Suddenly he runs off. Another camera picks up the story elsewhere, in another part of the wood. Julius put the bottle down on the floor, removed his glasses and rubbed his eyes. A cavernous yawn engulfed him. He shook his head and returned the glasses to his nose. Glancing at his wrist he read 'Philippe Sunday'. *Into the woods on the trail of CIRI, divided we fall united we stand, chain ourselves to the ancient oaks, Eva and Dany and all of the band.* What if he were to get arrested? Given the general situation the authorities could well have sent a detachment of police or army to patrol the site. It would be an obvious target for Rebex activists. Read all about it! 'British author and academic arrested'; 'KCL sacks rebel prof'; 'Environmental jihadists receive jail sentences.' His publishers would probably bring out a third edition of *Pandora's Mirror*, a potential succès de scandale on their books, but the Optimex connection was liable to go down the tubes, Harry D Crusoe might not want a revolutionary gracing the institute with his criminal presence. On the other hand all publicity is good publicity. It would be like having Julian Assange give a lecture.

I could write a prison diary. The Ballad of Lyon Gaol. It would present my final, my authoritative manifesto, the fruit of all my intellectual labours, interspersed with descriptions of prison food and fellow inmates. High philosophy conjoined with gritty verismo. 'I recall with particular vividness the evening on which I introduced René X, serial killer, to the concept of the noumenal world, and the light of enchanted recognition which suffused his pockmarked face.' It would sell millions, be translated into twenty languages. So fuck you, Hugh.

But they won't put you in jail, you are too old and you suffer from a psychological condition, the court will have mercy. A doctor will appear on your behalf as an expert witness. Maia will take the stand and confirm 'He is a sick man'. Philippe will confess to bamboozling you, to taking advantage of an ailing dementia victim. Shame on you Arentz! And from the prisoners' bench Eva will smile mournfully at you.

Maia saw a dead body floating in the river. In some obscure and complicated way this was connected with something else, with Albertine and with CIRI, if I applied myself I could untangle the crossed wires and arrive at … Carrots and sticks. A camera-flashing press conference. But now she is in her barn painting a picture of the Mother of God. All that blue! The young man and the young woman are listening to her as she explains what she is doing, why it is that Johnny is plummeting headlong out of the blue sky to hit the ground like a bolt of lightning in the foreground in the presence of Mary and bearing his extraordinary message, *He is alive, he is not dead.* The couple nod respectful heads, they are holding hands, fingers intertwined; eventually the girl asks: 'And did you love him?'

'Who?'

'Him.'

'Yes.'

Julius had a bit of a struggle getting out of his chair. Once he was standing it was all right but his head was swimming and his left hand trembled unaccountably. He moved carefully towards the window and opened it. Night air and yellow dustbins. Close the eyes, breathe in deeply. He could sense the mistral at play beyond the buildings bordering the courtyard, gusting down the narrow streets and rocking the moonlit plane trees in the Place aux Herbes. The rain from earlier in the day added a tangy freshness, in the sky a cloud scudded across the face of the moon, the stars were out. Toni, shall we take a walk together? Uzès is beautiful at night. I can show you the cathedral and the pavilion, we can sit side by side on the rim of the fountain in the Place aux Herbes and you can tell me all that you've been doing over the past five, ten, a hundred years. Come on.

He turned away from the window and walked past the TV screen, on which a player was being silently mobbed by his delirious teammates, picked up the key to his room and left. Down in the lift, through the lobby, past the girl at reception who is reading a magazine. Out of the doors, across the road. The mistral met him and walked with him. They went through the streets together, past bustling cafés and dark empty houses, from populous squares into deserted alleys, till they arrived in the Place du Duché, the mistral tousling his hair and even pushing him against a lamp post, what high spirits! He paused before the entrance to the duchy. Massive walls lowered, grey in the moonshine, and behind them the Bermonde Tower sat squatly against the sky. On the pitched roof of a smaller tower the Crussol crest was emblazoned. Parked cars shivered in the shadows. You see,

Toni, this is where I used to live several hundred years ago but they're turning it into a leper hospital now. You'd have liked it, there were lots of rooms, a magnificent tapestry of Alexander the Great, hunting trophies—we could take a look round now if you want, I think I've got my key on me, might have to bribe the guard... You'd rather not? Okay, let's walk on. Another day perhaps. If we go round the side here we can follow the defensive walls of the castle till we get to the Rue Amiral de Boueys, named after the Commander in chief of the allied Mediterranean navies during the First World War (thank you, little yellow pill)—yes here we are—and another tower rises up on your left, the Bishop's Tower, Tour de l'Évêque, the episcopal erection. Look, there's a cage at the top of it, that's where the bishop kept his eagle, it used to sing beautifully I remember: 'Whenever, whenever', except it was in French of course. On our left is the Rue Entre les Deux Tours.

I don't really know where I'm going. The cathedral was our goal, I think? This feels wrong. So much feels wrong and I don't know where I'm going. Not really. Don't know if I'm coming or going—neither apparently but what does it matter, we're having a nice walk aren't we, me and the mistral, he's a playful fellow, likes a bit of fun now and then. Sticks around for a week or two and everyone in the town goes mad, what jolly japes! Other things than wind can make you unbalanced, the loss of a loved one for example or just neurological degeneration, but to be driven mad by a wind is one of the more picturesque ways and it's less soul-destroying than the others, you're not all alone with your condition being watched by sympathetic outsiders, the wind is everywhere, everyone feels it, social madness binds the group together, think of the Nazis.

He clutched at some railings, a gust had nearly toppled him. Somebody laughed, probably himself. He staggered on and in a minute or two was in the Place aux Herbes. People were dotted around the square— although it was past midnight a couple of places were still open and after all it was peak season, more or less. Julius sat down at a table and ordered a Pernod. From across the square a bass voice shouted 'Milou! Viens ici!' Nearer to him a boy and a girl were seated, heads leaning together conspiratorially across a table, exchanging sweet nothings. The plane trees swayed and danced. Presently the Pernod arrived and with it a scrap of paper on a saucer, held in place by a rubber band.

'Santé,' Julius said aloud, lifting the glass to his lips.

'Et à vous,' returned the boy at the next table and his girlfriend looked round and smiled.

'J'ai besoin de santé en effet,' Julius informed them.

'Oui?'

'Yes. My health is, 'ow you say, none too good.'

'English?' enquired the girl.

'As a beefsteak. But I know these parts very well, Uzès and the surrounding country, very well indeed. At one time I resided in the chateau.'

The wind had got up strength and it blew away the last few words of his sentence.

'Pardon?'

'The chateau. I was duke there for a time. A benevolent master, I hope, and a loyal subject. My wife ...'

Old man Mistral was blowing hard now, he was obviously attempting to censor what Julius was saying. Julius carried on regardless.

'... happy period of time. It was not long before our union was blessed ...'

A glass broke nearby, the young man was getting to his feet. Julius raised his voice.

'... a sweet child, loved by all who knew her. Her mother, alas, passed away not long after the child was born, but her nurse cared for and looked after her as if it had been her own daughter. Her reward shall be in heaven. In her ninth year Cécile began to show symptoms of the condition which was ultimately to ... I employed the best doctors in the land, they tried everything, Dr Keller was wonderful but in the end, in the end it was the end. The end. You understand? Finis. We buried her in the family crypt. Later on a Requiem Mass was held in the cathedral, the king himself attending.'

People were leaving the square in twos and threes. A man was struggling to lower the awning outside a bar with a hooked pole. Leaves, napkins, crisp packets flew about; shouts were alternately muffled and magnified by the wind and Julius could hardly hear himself speak. The couple at the next table were gone. Hurrying across the square towards him came a waiter who nearly tripped over a running dog but managed to arrive just as Julius was finishing his Pernod. And suddenly, quite suddenly, the wind abated. The air was still and in the resulting silence a soft repeated sound could be heard, a sound like someone hiccupping. Julius felt an enormous weight in his chest. A light rain was falling and opposite him stood a man and a woman wearing black. Their heads were bowed. The hiccupping continued, it was louder now, and Julius looked up at the grey clouds with numb eyes and a numb heart wondering how such a thing as this was possible. Somebody was speaking, it was a monotonous sort of chant, Julius was unable to follow the words. His eyes dropped and took in once again the rectangular hole in the ground, the soil piled up beside it, the wooden box. Some men came forward and picked up the box with ropes and the hiccupping became a wailing and instinctively he clutched at Toni's hand, it was as if he were drowning, and as the box was lowered into the hole the water filled his lungs and he heard his own voice shouting *No* but the box continued on its way, it wanted to get to the bottom of the hole, get to the bottom and stay there. Soon they would throw earth over it. Finis, the end.

One of the pallbearers had jumped into the hole to check up on something, untwist a rope perhaps. Decorum demands. He ducked down and for a minute or so was invisible, the only sounds the patter of rain and Toni's sobbing, till first one hand and then the other appeared on the edge of the grave and between them there rose up like a head above a parapet the grinning face, ruddy and obscene, of a man wearing a baseball cap.

'Hello, Julius,' squeaked Hugh. 'You didn't think I'd turn up here of all places, now did you? And have we been having a *productive* summer? Writing anarchist pamphlets, so I hear? I do hope so . . .'

IX

MAIA KNEELED, ELBOWS RESTING ON the chair in front of her and hands clasped before her face. The sweet taste of communion wine was in her mouth. Per sanguinem tuum pretiosum redemisti mundum—you have redeemed the world, O Christ, have mercy on us sinners. Up in the west gallery the organ was playing and there was a shuffling queue of people in the central aisle, parishioners of Fournhac, those who still held God in their hearts, while the old priest mumbled and administered the sacrament, body and blood of our Lord Jesus Christ. Another Sunday, another miracle.

The congregation of St Hilaire was predominantly elderly but there were one or two families. A small girl in a pink dress approached the communion rail, encouraged by her mother. Behind her was her lankier brother in jeans and t-shirt—once upon a time he'd be got up in his Sunday best, hair combed and shoes polished, but youth's fashions didn't faze the priest, he was an old pro. The Eucharist itself was an outward and visible sign of inward and invisible grace so what went on in the boy's soul was bound to be hidden from view. She saw him raise his head a little as he received the wafer on his tongue. Then with God still in his mouth he stood up and returned, chewing, to his seat. The parents duly followed. When they got home from mass the family would sit down to enjoy a Sunday lunch of ham or chicken, Papa opening a nice bottle of vin rouge. At least she hoped they would. Meanwhile Béatrice and Lucien would presently be seeing to the lunches at *Les Pêcheurs*, squabbling in the kitchen and sharing gossip. On the dot of 12.30 Brian Decker would appear and install himself at the bar ready with his refrain: 'G and T please, Maia.'

The last communicant was returning to her seat, a small white-haired woman whom Maia knew only as Madame l'apicultrice. She sometimes brought jars of lavender-scented honey to the pub for sale; Maia placed the jars in a row on the window sill where they caught the light and turned a luminous orange. The old lady would come back a week later for her takings. She rarely spoke and was possibly quite deaf. It was all very rural, very self-sufficient, very Fournhac. Today Madame l'apicultrice would lunch alone in her dilapidated cottage on the edge of the village, spreading honey thickly on her buttered bread and sipping her eau de vie. After lunch she might take a nap or tend to her bees.

The congregation were standing for the last hymn. Maia got to her feet. She had a clear rich contralto voice and today she sang with more than usual warmth. To you be the glory, dear God. Thank you for coming among us and dwelling among us. Thank you for your generous bounty, for your everlasting goodness. And for answering our prayers.

For Johnny has visited.

Yes, he has visited. He has left signs and tokens, symbols in a language that only two people in the world understand. Footsteps in the sand. 'Hello there!' shouted the upside-down picture, 'I love you' whispered the sunflower. The beloved prankster has descended from the sky, impenitent grin on his adored adorable face, and my foolish heart sings like a bird.

...battez des mains at proclamez votre fête...

Yes, Johnny has visited at last. In person, in spirit, what does it matter? Alive or dead, what does it matter? He has come into my life again, has shown me his love, the love he once felt for me and so will always feel for me. She sang and the voices round her sang:

Que votre joie soit parfaite.

My joy is indeed perfect. I lift up my heart and sing.

The hymn came to an end. The old priest took a couple of paces forward and uttered the concluding words of the mass, *La messe est dite!* Without a break the organist launched into Bach's Toccata in F major. The people of Fournhac, spiritually sated, began to talk and exclaim among themselves, to stretch and scratch and shuffle. An old man with two walking sticks hooked one over the back of a chair so as to blow his nose, a teenager consulted her phone with studied casualness while her parents exchanged pleasantries with a neighbour. What had been united in a shared act of worship now broke up into its constituent parts, free-floating groups and autonomous individuals. The herd assembles, disperses, re-assembles, disperses . . .

But Maia remained in her seat. One more prayer before I go. With head bowed and hands clasped together she asked God *Please look after Julius.*

*

'Twist of lemon, match made in heaven.'

'That doesn't even rhyme.'

Brian drank from his glass then put it down with the words, 'Haven't you heard of assonance?'

Dave Gibbard snorted.

'Problem with you, Dave, is that you have no poetry in you. No Apollonian fire. It's because you're an engineer, I suppose. Good with nuts and bolts, less good at flights of fancy.'

'Is that your first?' responded Dave. 'You shouldn't have too many of those on an empty stomach. At your age . . .'

'Do stop bickering, you two,' said Maia.

'And by the way it's *civil* engineer.'

'Still no good at flights of fancy. I tell a lie, though— that stuff about the Suspicious Death of the Expert Witness was pretty imaginative, now wasn't it? How did it go again? Poor old Professor Boffin gets done in by the French equivalent of MI5, or possibly a poison dart from Rebex, and then pops up on the telly all apologetic. Conspiracy theory in tatters. Collapse of stout party.'

Dave Gibbard was humming a tune and looking the other way.

'Did they ever find out who the man in the river was?' asked Maia.

'Probably some homeless type. High on drugs, I expect.' Brian finished his gin and tonic (his third in fact) and turned his attention to the menu board.

An anonymous death. There must be dozens of them happening every day, people whose grip on life has grown steadily weaker until one day their fingers unclasp and they fall backwards, into the icy water, into the final night. Some with no friends or family, some with both but still alone, or who feel they are alone. But they are not alone, we are none of us alone, God holds us in the palm of his hand. Maia thought of the candle burning in St Hilaire.

'Embarras de choix,' commented Brian.

'Why don't you have what you always have?' Dave suggested. 'Wouldn't exactly be a flight of fancy but at least you'll be on safe ground.'

'Steak frites?' said Maia.

Brian shook his head. 'A change is as good as a rest— I'll have the Tarte Tatin. With chips.'

Dave snorted.

So the virology expert is still alive, thought Maia on her way to the kitchen. He merely went AWOL, as Dave would say. And now he can give his opinion to the committee: yes to the destruction of the forests or no to the destruction of the forests. As the case may be. Not that his opinion will necessarily be listened to. Powerful interests must be involved, there's always money to be made from such ventures. And once the planning has gone beyond a certain point, for the authorities to back out is for them to lose face, or think they've lost face. As if pride and vanity were virtues!

In the kitchen she found Béatrice more than usually flustered. It seemed that Lucien had phoned in sick at the last minute. Maia offered to help. 'And the customers?' Béatrice demanded. 'They can cope without me for ten minutes,' said Maia. 'The sky won't fall down. What shall I do?' Béatrice tasked her with chopping vegetables. Soon her calm was restored. The two women laughed and chatted; a couple of onions later and the atmosphere was quite companionable. In the old days Maia would be standing here laughing and chatting with Johnny as they cooked up whatever could be microwaved come lunchtime, basic fare for a basic clientele. The kitchen was smaller then, the possibilities fewer. It would have been nice to have Johnny there with them now, cracking jokes or juggling tomatoes.

But of course he is here, she thought.

*

Harry D Selkirk came downstairs whistling something that could have been Danny Boy. He was in the best of spirits. The immediate future, having been shadowy and indeterminate, had clicked into focus. Julius Durward was in the bag. Now he could indulge in more ambitious plans: seminars could be arranged, invitations sent out, the website could be handed over to a full-time curator (if that was the word) and media outlets approached.

The Optimex Foundation was going to be put on the map.

It was eight o'clock in the morning and the birds were singing in the garden but Selkirk's footsteps were taking him to the library, there to contemplate the riches of the human intellect and more specifically to reread the closing pages of *Pandora's Mirror*, the part of the book that always inspired him with a sense of infinite and astounding possibilities. In this coda or peroration the author seemed by pulling a hidden drawstring to reveal a vast and unexpected panorama full of joy and strife, and if that wasn't a prediction of technological and political perfection then he, Selkirk, was a Chinaman. The inaugural lecture could very well carry on where this vision left off. Maybe Travis should hint as much to the professor.

The book sat in its usual place on the little table by his favourite armchair. Selkirk picked it up: a substantial paperback, spine well creased, with a swirling grey and red cover design. On the back was a puff from the New York Times: 'This book is at once a catharsis and a reckoning. Durward has anatomized the malaise of a culture—our own.'

'Bullshit,' muttered Selkirk not for the first time and turned to page 380.

There was a knocking at the open library door.

'Morning, Nico,' said Selkirk without turning round. 'I'll have my coffee here if that's okay.'

No response. Selkirk finished the paragraph and when, vaguely disturbed by Nico's silence, he looked over to the doorway he saw no one there. Thinking nothing of it he walked over to one of the windows for better illumination and continued his reading. The grandfather clock, which was fast, chimed the half hour.

> *The views of a man like Philippe Arentz receive both confirmation and confutation from the current European developments. Different tendencies within Western society point in different directions. The statement is a truism. Hence a just assessment of our predicament may have to mirror the paradoxicality of what it attempts to depict and in so doing invite the charge of incoherence. Arentz is no friend of Hegel, but in the end he and those like him might have to admit that . . .*

This was one of those passages Selkirk preferred to skim-read. He didn't see the point of bringing in the ideas of this or that French intellectual. Better to cut to the chase. Turning the page he resumed at:

> *. . . a substantive notion of human happiness still eludes us. Our attempts to articulate such a notion falter repeatedly. And yet when we come across happiness, say in the games and laughter of children, it can seem the most obvious thing in the world. Should politicians be required to mix with the under-tens? It is a genuine question . . .*

Selkirk chuckled. There was nothing to beat the English sense of humour. Dry as a bone. He imagined Durward's deadpan delivery and the murmured pleasure of his audience, an occasional explosion of laughter from the back row. 'Required to mix with the under-tens'! Brilliant, love it. And at the end the ovation, the stamping of feet... headlines in the quality press: 'Durward delights his audience', 'Auspicious start for global institute'. How much time would Durward need to write it? Three months? Six months? Selkirk was ignorant of the working habits of academics. If he offered £5000 up-front, the remainder to be paid on delivery, that might act as a spur to the professor's creativity. He'd ask Travis.

> *A time may come when sprightly 100-year-olds can be seen jogging round Central Park, when 24-hour infotainment is beamed into every room of every house, and when sleeping bags in doorways disappear as quickly and inexplicably as they appear...*

Here we are, the last act, the grand finale. 'A time may come'—I mean to live long enough to see that time, I can tell you. Some words of Nietzsche's were knocking around in his head: *Let the festival...*

'Your coffee, Mr Selkirk.'

Nico had materialised noiselessly and was standing beside the little table holding a tray.

'Thank you, Nico, just put it there.'

Nico transferred cafetiére, cup, saucer and milk jug from tray to table. His employer observed him with satisfaction. Best handyman and manservant in the state of Virginia, clean, efficient and reliable. It's been a few years since his last pay rise, mused Selkirk, maybe I should give him another one. He'd only spend it on cig-arettes, mind you.

'Say, Nico.'

'Yes, sir?'

'I guess you could use a pay rise one of these days?'

An odd sort of smile appeared on Nico's face. 'That won't be necessary, Mr Selkirk. You're very kind. But it won't be necessary.'

'Whatever you say,' said Selkirk, mildly surprised at this rebuff. 'But if you change your mind ...'

Nico bowed as if to say 'You may count on my sincere appreciation, sir.'

When he had gone Selkirk settled down in his arm-chair with his book. He read a few more pages then put it down and poured himself some coffee. It would be interesting to meet Durward, of course, but he was sure his present plan was the best plan. He already had a vivid mental picture of the author of *Pandora's Mirror* and was dimly aware that an encounter with the real thing might destroy that picture, for which (since it was the offspring of his mind) he felt a parental tender-ness. His own version of Julius Durward might after all be superior in many ways to the flesh and blood Julius Durward. That was a phenomenon he had experienced a few times in his life.

Sipping his coffee Selkirk fell to reminiscence. He had first heard of *Pandora's Mirror* when a programme about it was broadcast on the radio, one of those late night shows devoted to book reviews and cultural chit-chat. He'd undressed for bed and had taken his sleeping pill and was half-dozing in the chair in his bedroom waiting for the drowsiness to take hold of him, it being not so long since Doreen had died. With sleep came oblivion, but sleep couldn't be commanded—or rather it could be commanded with the assistance of temazepam and background radio talk. Cajoled, perhaps. Anyway, there he was, letting the benzo do its work and trying not to think about his late wife when some commentator on the programme began describing what sounded like a combination of history lesson, dream narrative and religious manifesto. Perhaps it was the effect of his altered state of consciousness, but for whatever reason Selkirk found himself drawn into this strange new world of ideas, this alien but sympathetic mindset with its parables and prognostications. The phrase *reading the future in the past* fell from the commentator's lips and lodged itself in Selkirk's mind like an incubus. Next day the phrase came to him again, pregnant with meaning, as he strolled through the garden, and its undiminished force was clear evidence that the impressions of the previous evening were not just the temazepam talking.

'Hell, no,' said Selkirk in his armchair. He shook his head for emphasis and the library rolled like a ship. Whoa . . . Funny, that—almost as if recalling the effects of benzoes could give you a flashback. He did feel a little drowsy. Well, that's how it all started and it wasn't long before he'd bought the book off Amazon with Durward's signature on the inside cover. He read the whole thing in two sittings, taking notes. Quickly recognised Durward for the genius that he was. Hell, yes.

The library rolled again. He tried to bring it to a standstill, with moderate success. Experimentally he moved his head from side to side. Interesting. A pleasurable enough sensation but tinged with nausea. No doubt it would pass. He returned to his train of thought.

In a way it's true to say that I would never have fallen under Julius Durward's spell if Doreen hadn't died. If she'd lived we'd be cuddled up in bed together, I wouldn't be listening to the radio trying to forget all about her. Cuddled up with Pandora in my hand. In my head. Whoa … This is like—like floating. Up, up … Close eyes, open eyes. That ceiling light is so close I could touch it, kiss her almost. And down there my fossils are swimming through murky water: hello fossils. I can hear, I can hear the ringing of bells and somewhere a long way off a tinkling sound, something breaking—coffee cup –

*

In the Place aux Herbes a man was going around picking up litter with a trash picker. Overnight the wind had died down; in its wake it left broken glass, bits of paper and plastic, one or two overturned chairs, an atmosphere of exhausted revelry. The mistral had been at play.

Philippe scanned the scene. He had come from the Hotel Jaurès. The receptionist had shrugged her shoulders: the night porter was gone and she'd only just come on duty herself so couldn't be of any assistance. Philippe asked her to phone Durward in his room. There was no response. To his further request she replied that alas, monsieur, it is not the policy of the hotel to enter the rooms of guests without their permission. 'Je regrette que ce n'est pas possible.' And again she shrugged her pretty shoulders.

The man with the trash picker bent over to pick up a chair and planted it somewhere at random where it could fend for itself. Philippe made his way across the square, past the sleeping fountain and under a plane tree to where Julius was slumped over a café table. His head rested on his arms and his face was buried in the crook of an elbow. Philippe stood over him. Oh Durward... He placed a hand on Julius's shoulder. Raising his head and speaking in a husky but distinct voice Julius said, 'You could have tripped over that dog.' He blinked a few times; there were shadows under his eyes. Then: 'Hello, Philippe.'

'Hello, Durward. Have you been here all night? I'm surprised you weren't blown across the square.'

Julius rubbed his face with both hands and leant back in his chair. Mussed hair, rumpled jacket. Philippe looked around for the litter-picker but he had gone indoors.

'Let's have breakfast, you look as if you need it. You stay here and I'll find something.'

'All right,' said Julius and closed his eyes. Philippe went off in the direction of a bistro he'd passed on his way there. Before long he returned carrying a brown paper bag from which he produced two coffees and two toasted sandwiches.

'Protein, caffeine, carbohydrate and salt,' he announced, pulling up a chair. 'Benedictus benedicat.'

'Per Jesum Christum dominum nostrum,' finished Julius. 'Is today Sunday?'

'Today is Sunday.'

The two men tucked in. Julius was very hungry. He ate his cheese and tomato toastie with relish. As he did so a thought began to take shape in his mind. If today was Sunday…

'I'm meant to be meeting somebody. I've written it down.' He examined his wrist. 'I'm meeting Philippe Arentz. We're going to be planning something quite important.'

'What would that be?'

'Something to do with a virology research centre.' He drank some coffee. 'You know—like Porton Down. Philippe's anarchist principles lead him to take a very dim view of the whole business and I have to say I agree with him. The destruction of an ancient forest…'

'Julius.' Philippe had taken hold of his arm and was looking hard at him. 'Julius. Who am I? Who are you talking to now?'

From twenty yards away the litter-picker, emerging from a doorway, observed a pair of gentlemen at a café table staring at one another. They appeared frozen. A breeze passed through the Place aux Herbes breathing life into the taller of the two: he freed himself from the other's grip and got unsteadily to his feet. The other rose also.

'But why all this fuss, Philippe? Anyway isn't it time we were making a move?' Julius looked at his watch. 'My car's parked near the hotel. Come on.'

Philippe sat down again. He stroked his head. 'Finish your breakfast, Durward. We have plenty of time.'

With fading interest the litter-picker saw the taller man pick up his sandwich, sit down and continue eating.

The sun had risen now above the tops of the buildings and one side of the square was warm with reflected light. Philippe and Julius sat on the other side, within the shadow. Human beings were beginning to appear, sauntering or walking briskly, tourists or residents, beckoned by pleasure or by business. A thrush sang at some spot above their heads. Further along a café was opening. Uzès was waking up, yawning and stretching and girding its loins for another day.

'Just to recap,' said Philippe between mouthfuls, 'we're going to drive to Valliguières, then walk. It's about four kilometres to the site. I'll phone the others to tell them we're on our way; they've set up camp nearby. It's a Sunday so there won't be any work going on and they haven't got as far as employing guards. There's a fence but you can get through it. Dany plans to build a tunnel eventually.'

Julius listened and nodded.

'I think you should take notes. Have you a pen and paper? If not I can supply you. I know you don't use modern technology. You need to be able to write as a witness, as somebody who is acquainted with the body on which the wound is to be inflicted. You will be able to meet and talk with those risking their freedom in order to protect the forest and fight against the assassins and the disease-mongers. In short, the purpose of the visit is to provide you with material and with authenticity. A writer needs both if he is to persuade.'

Julius was smiling. 'Really you should be writing this pamphlet, old chap. Haven't you written it already, in fact? In your head, I mean? Of course I don't mind appending my name if you think that'll help. But I don't think I could do any better than you, your style is so lofty and poetical...'

'We can talk about all that later. My main concern now is that you're up to this. We're going to be hiking through woods, mainly uphill. As far as I can see you haven't had a proper night's sleep. We're neither of us young. I don't want to have to call an air ambulance, that sort of publicity wouldn't appeal to my colleagues at all.'

'Your fellow anarchists, you mean?'

'D'you think you're well enough to do this, Durward? I need to know.'

'Well enough?' Julius began to laugh. 'Well enough? But weren't you aware, Philippe—I'm going mad, your old friend Julius Durward is going insane. Fortunately, however, the people around me are also mad by and large, so it doesn't show so much. You're rather mad yourself, you'll surely admit.'

Philippe considered him. He was weighing the pros and cons. It was too late to abort the project now and if he ended up writing the exposé himself he'd got

Durward's permission to bring it out under his name. That was the main thing.

'Well, perhaps you'll let me drive,' he said.

*

The journey to Valliguières was uneventful. Julius dozed in the passenger seat while the car radio relayed a stream of news bulletins about the rioting in Paris and elsewhere. The army had been brought in and rumours were spreading of a possible general strike. The president was to address the nation later in the day. Philippe switched channels, got a quiz show and turned the radio off.

They left the car in a car park near the centre of the village. 'Very pretty,' Julius said as they walked past the mairie. 'We could have lunch here.' Philippe ignored the remark. Soon they were following an irrigation canal that led out of Valliguières to the north, skirting vineyards and garden plots in which hollyhocks jostled with runner beans. Ahead of them in the distance were thickly wooded hills. Durward appeared to be none the worse for a night spent slouched at a café table. He walked easily, even strode, commenting from time to time on their surroundings or on such events of French history as seemed to him relevant. His mood was buoyant. After a quarter of an hour, when they'd left Valliguières behind them, Philippe got out his phone and dialled. A brief conversation ensued of which Julius overheard only *pas longtemps*. The sun had disappeared and the temperature had dropped a couple of degrees;

this made for easier walking but Philippe didn't like the look of the grey clouds approaching from behind. They weren't dressed for a downpour. However once inside the woods they'd at least have some cover.

And before long they were inside the woods, trudging through trackless bracken and stumbling over tree roots. The trees were mainly oaks, interspersed with beeches and eucalyptuses. On their barks sat alien-looking encrustations of grey-brown fungi bigger than a man's hand. Among the branches above their heads invisible creatures darted or flew, dislodging an occasional acorn which would fall to earth with a muted *flum*. A rich loamy smell rose up from the ground, prehistoric and intoxicating. They were scaling a hill and it wasn't long before Philippe was out of breath; Julius on the other hand seemed invigorated. He looks younger, thought Philippe wiping the sweat from his face. He moves like a man half his age.

'Not so fast, Durward. We have plenty of time.'

Julius stopped and looked back at his friend. 'The air is good here, don't you think? It must be rich in oxygen.'

'Is that what it is.'

'You smoke too many cigarettes, Philippe. I don't suppose you exercise a great deal either, do you, being a sedentary academic.'

Philippe caught up with him. 'Aren't you a sedentary academic yourself?'

Julius turned and moved off. 'There are boar in these woods,' was all he said.

Eventually the incline lessened and they were walking more or less on the flat. The already dim light had grown dimmer and a new noise could be heard among the noises of the forest, the patter of rain. It wasn't heavy but it was steady. 'Merde,' muttered Philippe, his thoughts turning to mud. The shoes he was wearing were hardly suitable for hiking but then he didn't possess any shoes that were. He was, as Julius had pointed out, a sedentary academic. Louise would sometimes tease him for his pot belly but he was scared of bikes and going to the gym was beneath him. His own view was that the cult of health was just another sickness of the age, an expression of man's futile yearning for immortality.

Ahead of him Julius had just negotiated a fallen branch, lifting his long legs over it almost absent-mindedly. Philippe when he reached it realised he would need to tackle the object with more care. He planted one foot on the branch and half-jumped. The branch slithered underneath him as if trying to escape and he lurched forwards, landing awkwardly and feeling a jab of pain in his left ankle. For a minute he stood with his hands on his knees, head bent, breathing hard. When he had recovered himself he set off after Julius and at once realised that the pain was there to stay—he had sprained his ankle. Swearing and limping Philippe began to ask himself in earnest whether this forest outing was such a good idea. He could have just described the place to Durward, after all. And they were going to have to walk all the way back to Valliguières.

'Durward!' he shouted, 'Hold on, will you? I've twisted my ankle.'

Julius came back to join him.

'Is it bad?'

'Bad enough.'

Without a word Julius drew Philippe's arm around his shoulders to support him and they walked on in a tottery embrace. It took a while for them to settle into a sustainable rhythm and at certain points the difference in the men's heights posed its own problems. Philippe's left shoulder began to feel numb. A couple of times he asked Julius to stop so he could put some weight on the ankle and test it: it was no better, no worse. Julius began telling him some story about a wounded troubadour and Philippe was wondering how much longer they'd be walking like this when from quite nearby came a high-pitched whistle. They stopped and the whistle was repeated. Philippe put two fingers into his mouth and whistled in return, then pointed into the trees and said, 'That way.' They changed tack and a moment later a human figure emerged from the shadows which turned out to be Laurent. He was wearing khaki and his face was daubed with smears of green and brown. When he saw them he waved and beckoned them to follow. 'Not too fast,' grunted Philippe but Laurent probably didn't hear him.

The trees were thinning out a little and the sound of the rain seemed to become deeper and louder. Philippe's shoulder was now hurting as much as his ankle. 'Let me walk this last bit on my own,' he said. Julius complied.

His glasses had steamed up and he paused to wipe them with a handkerchief. Laurent had almost disappeared from view. The undergrowth was thicker here and the two men advanced slowly, wading through ferns, clothes sodden and shoes caked with leaves and mud. Finally and to Philippe's relief they saw tents ahead of them; they were pitched in a sort of clearing, two grey ones and a third that was a dirty green. Laurent and another person stood waiting patiently in the rain for the arrival of the visitors.

'Hello, professor,' said Laurent as Julius approached. 'Thank you for coming.' They shook wet hands. 'I hope you will find the experience interesting. This is Sophie.'

'Hello, Sophie.'

Sophie was short and wore an oversized cagoule with a hood but Julius was able to make out a pair of glasses and a toothy smile.

'I really think we should get under cover,' Philippe said.

'Of course. Please come into this tent over here, there is a gas fire.' Laurent guided them to the dirty green tent and the three men entered crouching in single file. Sophie evaporated somewhere. Once inside Laurent hunted out a box of matches. While he fumbled with these Philippe, sitting on the ground sheet, removed his left shoe and sock and took to massaging his ankle. 'Is it swollen?' asked Julius. He was sitting on a camp chair, knees sticking out. Philippe made an ambiguous noise. He turned to Laurent and asked him in French if there was any brandy on the premises. Laurent said he would enquire. The rain drummed down on the roof of the tent, a soothing soporific sound blending somehow with the heat of the fire which was beginning to envelop them. Julius was reminded of camping holidays from his childhood.

Outside the tent somebody laughed. The three of them looked towards the tent door and saw the flap thrust aside by a man's hand. Through the aperture a head appeared, rubicund and glistening with rain, black hair plastered over its forehead.

Philippe raised a hand in greeting then turned to his friend: 'Julius, meet Max.'

The head bowed, smiling.

X

'PHILIPPE HAS TOLD ME A lot about you. He thinks you can help us in our fight.'

Max sat cross-legged on the ground sheet. He wore an army issue waterproof jacket, jeans and trainers. His large powerful-looking hands were folded in his lap and on the little finger of the right hand sat a bulbous platinum ring. Julius estimated his age as being somewhere between thirty-five and forty-five. A faint scar ran from the corner of his mouth to the middle of his cheek.

'I'm not a reading man myself and don't know your book but I understand it contains many good things.'

The accent was hard to place: east European? The Balkans? It seemed to have disparate elements, was redolent of everywhere and nowhere.

'I haven't looked at it myself for years,' said Julius. 'I've mostly forgotten what it says.'

'But that's not the point, is it,' said Philippe, who had stretched out and was leaning on one elbow. 'The point isn't what you have written but what you will write.'

'Quite so,' agreed Max. He smiled enigmatically. Laurent was fiddling with the gas fire, adjusting the temperature. The camouflage paint glistened on his cheeks. It'll start running soon, thought Julius, his face will look like a Jackson Pollock.

The tent was a large one and the four men occupied the space comfortably. A variety of smells mingled: damp clothes drying, sweaty feet, propane gas. Outside the rain continued to fall. 'You must both be hungry,' said Max, 'we'll get you something to eat, then we can proceed to the purpose of your visit, Professor Durward. Perhaps by that stage it will have stopped raining.'

'Do call me Julius. Yes, I'd like a bite to eat. Thanks.' Hours or days ago he had breakfasted on toasted sandwiches at a café table in the Place aux Herbes.

'Philippe asked if we had any brandy,' remarked Laurent. Max raised an eyebrow and Philippe, pointing to a naked foot, explained: 'For my ankle.'

Ten minutes later the food had appeared—bread, cheese, gherkins, fruit and a slab of chocolate. Philippe drank his brandy from a paper cup while the others stuck to coffee out of a thermos. They were joined by Sophie, the hood of whose cagoule was thrown back to reveal spikey green and orange hair. Julius spread some gorgonzola on a hunk of bread and hummed to himself.

'Philippe will have explained the nature of the building site you'll be inspecting,' said Max. 'I'd be interested in your opinion of that. A lot of controversy surrounds this project, many pros and cons have been aired. Perhaps you'll tell me where you yourself stand, what sorts of arguments you'd muster if, for example, you were be-ing interviewed. What would you say to someone who argued that the authorities have every right to build a scientific research centre of this kind? It's for the good of humanity, after all.'

'I'd ask why it had to be in the middle of this forest,' replied Julius, chewing.

'So as not to be near human habitations.'

'Which is an admission that the research in question is potentially dangerous.'

'So is a nuclear power plant.'

'I don't like them either.'

'But the French do like them. You'll need a better argument.'

Max sat cross-legged, Buddha-like. Occasionally he fingered his platinum ring. Julius was silent, finally coming out with 'This is good cheese' addressed to no one in particular. He spread some more gorgonzola on his bread and offered the pack to Max, who held up a hand in polite refusal.

'Max is vegan,' said Sophie with a sort of vicarious pride.

'He is opposed to the oppression of cows,' elaborated Philippe. Max ignored him and continued: 'Why *not* have a virology institute? The Chinese have them.'

'Bugger the Chinese,' said Julius. 'These forests…these forests…' He passed a hand across his brow. 'In 1665, the duke of Uzès held a birthday party here, I mean it was a hunting party to celebrate his wife's birthday, twenty or so lords and ladies on horseback, plus retainers, plus dogs.'

'Dogs?' repeated Max.

'Yes, dogs…'

'Most interesting, I'm sure. The aristocracy with its menagerie in tow, a pretty sight. But why are you talking to us about dogs? Or horses? Do you want to tell us about anteaters too? Are we here to discuss our favourite animals? Is that what British intellectuals do?'

No one said anything. Laurent was smirking.

'But you're the vegan, Max,' Philippe pointed out.

Max turned to him with narrowed eyes. 'If you're this man's minder you should be minding him better. I had been led to expect something with ammunition in it. Didn't you promise that?'

Philippe shrugged. 'Julius is tired out. So am I. We both just slogged here through the rain and mud, and now we're recuperating. He didn't sleep much last night either.' He finished his brandy.

Max bent his gaze upon Julius, who was staring at the ground, then slapped his thighs with both hands and said with sudden good humour, 'Well, gentlemen, we shall see what we shall see. It is time to plan the day ahead. And if I am not mistaken—' He raised a finger. The drumming of the rain had dwindled to a pitter-patter on the roof of the tent. Max's warm smile embraced the company.

When they'd finished eating Sophie cleared the things away. Some of the old hierarchies survived among the Rebex radicals, it seemed. Julius offered to help but Sophie shook her head smiling. Philippe spent some time putting his shoes on, grunting with pain as the left shoe was forced over the ankle; Laurent stood up and stretched. Max had already left the tent saying that he was going to return with a couple of spare cagoules for the visitors. He must have found them hard to locate for he took longer than expected and by the time he was back the rain had started up again.

'When I go back to Paris I'm going to buy myself three new pairs of shoes,' announced Philippe.

'You need trainers,' advised Sophie. 'Or proper boots.'

'So young but so wise,' he responded, dimples in his cheeks. Sophie's face flushed beneath the orange and green thatch and she made for the tent door, crouching and pulling the hood of her cagoule over her head.

'These are the same size, I'm afraid,' said Max, handing the spare cagoules to Philippe. 'Your socks may get a little damp,' he added to Julius. Then he too left the tent, followed by Laurent. The gas fire had been turned off; its hiss gave way to a sputtering diminuendo which in turn gave way to silence.

'How are you feeling, Durward?'

'Oh, fine,' said Julius. 'Ready for the hunt.' Stooping, he pulled the cagoule over his head and thrust his arms out. 'Where is that man from?'

'Max? He's a citizen of the world. A true cosmopolitan. His father was Syrian, his mother was Dutch, I believe. God knows where he grew up; the North Pole, possibly. He's done some effective work for us, doesn't mind transgressing legal boundaries where necessary. Knows the right sort of people.'

'Criminals, you mean?'

'According to a certain perspective. According to another perspective it's the makers not the breakers of the laws who ought to be punished. But you know my views on these matters. Are you ready?' Philippe was tightening the drawstring of his hood. 'Maybe you could lend me a discreet hand when we're outside.'

'And which one of you is in charge?'

Philippe gave him an indulgent smile. 'Really, Durward, it's as if you'd forgotten what *anarchism* means. If it helps you to categorise us, you can think of me as the elder statesman and Max as the commando. For what it's worth.'

Max led the way. They left the tents and the clearing behind them, plunging into the forest along a muddy track on which a chaos of superimposed footprints bore witness to journeys backwards and forwards, to all the busy activity of a guerrilla army preparing for an offensive—reconnoitring, surveying, establishing a presence. They had left base camp and were heading for the front line. There the enemy would soon be initiating its filthy war against nature. Julius recalled Max's words: *We shall see what we shall see.* So we shall, he thought. I'll need that pen and paper. Philippe promised me some, didn't he? Philippe was a yard or two ahead of him, the back of his cagoule lurching gently each time his left foot touched the ground. The path was too narrow for Julius to assist him but he seemed to be managing; at any rate they weren't falling far behind Max. Laurent brought up the rear, invisible at his back.

France was in turmoil. Civil war loomed. And Julius was embedded in a gang of insurrectionists led by a shadowy figure with contacts in the underworld, embedded where he could observe and report on their readiness for action. He wondered what sort of action it would be. Sabotage, violence? Or self-sacrifice? Perhaps he wouldn't find out, perhaps he'd just get a demonstration of wire-cutting along with an environmentalist lecture. But you never knew, they might invite him to stick around for some fireworks. Then he'd be witnessing history. For once it wouldn't be Durward going back in time—history would have caught up with Durward. If you stay still long enough it'll get to you eventually. It was the precise nature of the fireworks that eluded him, that being the problem with living history as opposed to studying it.

All this was illusion, however: the fact is, one lives in the present, which is a boat on a river with its windows pointing backwards, and the windows misting over. From within the enclosure of his hood Julius as he walked listened to a symphony of polyester and rain. The grey rustling din of the fabric and the water, pulsing to the rhythm of his footfall, made a wall of sound which to some extent separated him from the others: if they spoke he didn't hear them, but they probably didn't speak. Philippe would be enclosed in a similar private sound world. Each occupied his own cell now, it was a reversion to the solipsism of the womb, rhythmic throb of placental blood dinning in one's ears, nothing to do nothing to think, no past, only an indefinite future… He stumbled on a tree root, one arm flailed and Laurent had caught him. Julius straightened slowly, looked into the eyes of the brown-green face and smiled. For a moment the boy smiled back, then it was as if something inside him was switched off. The impassive stare returned and he gestured forwards. Julius obeyed.

The next thing he knew he had collided with Philippe, running into the back of him. The column had come to a standstill. 'Sorry,' he blurted, then looking ahead he saw the hole in the ground. The hole was huge. They viewed it through a gap in a wire fence, this gap corresponding to a portion that had been roughly cut away and now hung there lopsided like a door falling off its hinges. Near the centre of the hole, on the basin floor, stood a mechanical digger at rest. Puddles of water surrounded it, grey surfaces stippled by rain. A pile of duckboards over to one side awaited distribution across the muddy ground. The protective tarpaulin had been pulled off and lay stupidly in a heap next to them. On the other side of the hole from where Julius and the others stood, a hundred metres away, you could see that trees were being uprooted, felled, eliminated, eventually to be reduced to sawdust or if lucky recycled. The hole was only going to get bigger.

'Voilà,' shouted Max. 'Behold the cesspit.'

Julius stepped forward, passed Max through the gap in the fence and stopped by the crater's rim. The war on nature had already begun. For a long time he stood looking. It was only when he turned round to ask a question that he saw they had been joined by some other people, four figures materialising from he didn't know where, three men and a woman. Eva and Dany he recognised, the other two were new.

'Bonjour,' he said.

'Bonjour,' smiled Eva. The others weren't smiling.

*

Meadowlarks were singing in the trees that bordered the artificial lake and the reflected sky was cloudless and still. Nico pushed off from the landing stage. As the rowing boat cut through the water he settled himself on the thwart and took up the oars. The bag with its contents was shoved into the stern of the boat, its zip fastener nearly but not quite closed.

The artificial lake had been one of Mr Selkirk's first improvements after moving into The Vines. Tons of earth had been removed, thousands of gallons of water pumped in. This was all before Nico's time, of course; he knew of it only through Mr Selkirk's many tellings, from which he learnt among other things how deep the lake was and that it was populated by various fish, including some Koi carp and an ageing pike. It was Nico's job on occasion to replenish the stock, which meant a three-hour round trip to a wholesale aquatic supplier in Richmond whose flirty big-busted receptionist provided some additional incentive. Pike were carnivorous, he reminded himself. Maybe Koi carp were too. He wasn't sure.

Nico drew in the oars and let the boat drift. He was approaching the end of a narrow wooden pier carpeted with green algae. Lighting a cigarette he rehearsed mentally the steps that were to be taken. After this job he would return to the house, clean some surfaces in the library and make a phone call. Nothing drastic in the library, just spilt coffee and a few bits of broken china, it should only take five or ten minutes. He had considered finishing the business with a blow to the head (skull crumpling under stone or iron) but that would have risked blood, and a drop of blood can get a man hanged. Or imprisoned for life. In any case, the idea of such violence repelled him. If the shock of cold water momentarily revived the old man his sufferings would be short-lived; only a brute would forestall that possibility by raising his hand against his fellow creature as Cain did to Abel. This way, sleep would blend with death. 'Enough to knock out an elephant' was the phrase the man had used as he handed over the little bottle in exchange for Nico's dollars on the evening when the two of them sat in a dimly lit corner of a downtown bar.

He took a last drag on his cigarette then flung it away. The butt hit the water and sank. A heron flew by overhead, great wings flapping—its shadow glided beneath it across the lake. Nico leant forward and pulled the bag towards him. Carrying and dragging it the half mile from the house to the lake hadn't been so difficult, not for a man of Nico's strength. He had taken care to fold the body up, knees to chest, lest the dose had proved fatal and rigor mortis set in; a rigid object needs to be compact for optimum manoeuvrability. It had lain in that foetal position on the polished floor next to the armchair in the library while he went down to the basement to get the bag: a double sleeping bag stuffed into a dusty and cobweb-infested cardboard box. Selkirk must have taken it with him on camping trips as a young man.

The image of the body on the library floor suddenly struck Nico as comical and he laughed aloud. So this is what you've come to, old man. You thought you'd live for ever, didn't you, with a brief interlude in an ice-box, and now you're just a dead weight in a zipped-up bag whose destiny is to feed the fishes, unless you get dredged up, the evident victim of a self-inflicted senile mishap. Oh, you'll get your resurrection all right, we all will. God sees to that, God who made Leviathan whose breath kindleth coals and whose eyes are like the eyelids of the morning, you fool, you dotard. Man is arrogant (he heaved the bag onto the edge of the boat), man puffs himself up, he strives to be god-like and that is why he falls, that is why he fell, to taste of sin and death. Sin and death: see how the one leads to the other, Selkirk. Yet although I have been sinned against I forgive you. I am still your faithful servant. Who else would perform for you this final office?

Clutching the bag tight, with one hand poised on the zip pull, Nico closed his eyes and spoke: 'As we commit the body of our brother Harry to the deep, grant him peace and tranquillity until that day when he and all who...'

From the aperture in the zip came a low grating noise. Nico stopped. The grating continued—guttural, insistent. Then, unmistakably, an intake of breath. Nico felt something pushing into his ribs.

'Amen.'

He grasped the zip pull and tugged on it. It moved a few swift inches down the zip then came to a halt, stuck or obstructed by something. With a curse he yanked at it as the guttural noises became louder but the zip pull remained obstinately static. Close it a bit then open it again, he thought, that way you'll pass over the obstruction. The double movement worked and now the zip was opening up and the bag was changing shape—it was as if the thing was about to give birth. But what followed was something much more like the blind fumblings of sex, bodies tangled in a horrible struggling intimacy... Two feet emerged, one of them missing a shoe—spindly legs, a bony elbow. Last out, the tousled bobbing head, one eye open. As he grappled with this rag doll Nico felt a cold hand brush his cheek and his gorge rose. At last there came a splash, ripples of water and bubbles coming up to the surface. As the concentric ripples travelled across the lake the bubbles kept coming. He peered over the edge of the boat and made out through the remarkably clear water (a matter of pride to Mr Selkirk) a receding shape from which emerged the stream of bubbles, reaching up to the surface of the lake like a lifeline. *Catch hold of it, Nico, pull hard, help me out of here.* Nico shut his eyes tight. His hands gripped the side of the boat and he repeated to himself that a thin human body in fresh water will sink not float, sink not float. After counting down from ten he looked again into the water. The shape was much smaller now and merging with the murk and shadows. Soon it had disappeared.

He sat back, kicked the empty bag away from him and fumbled for a cigarette. All right. Job done. His fingers were sweaty, it took him a while to get the lighter to work. After a couple of deep puffs he left the cigarette in his mouth and began to row back to the old wooden landing stage from which, fifty summers ago, two newly-weds had jumped laughing into the water.

*

The sound of rain came through the open French windows and Travis got himself another beer from the mini fridge. Kelly was curled up on the sofa reading a book. It had been raining since mid-morning.

'How's it going?' said Travis. He threw himself into an armchair.

Kelly looked up. 'Interesting. Kind of strange. What the critics call *unclassifiable*. That Philippe guy has just turned up, sounding off about everything. Did you know it was him when we met him with Julius?'

'You mean did I realise Arentz was a character from *Pandora's Mirror*? Sure.'

'You didn't mention it.'

'I thought it might embarrass the professor. Plus I wanted to see how he talked in real life.'

'The same as in the book, right?'

'Uh-huh. Durward does a good pen portrait. I can't really figure out what they see in each other. I mean, Arentz is such a loudmouth, he thinks he's right about everything.'

'Julius also likes lecturing people.'

'Yeah, but he's not an egoist like Arentz. He's more, somehow...'

'What?'

Travis hunted for the word. 'Vulnerable. Or something.'

'You're right. That's quite perceptive, Trav. For a guy it has to be said you're quite sensitive.'

Travis blew a raspberry.

She said, 'I wonder if the lecture will be like the book.'

'God knows. I'll be happy just so long as it happens. As far as I'm concerned he can talk about the habits of armadillos. The key thing is that Uncle Harry gets his inaugural lecture.'

'Do you love your uncle, Trav?'

'Love him?' Travis pulled a face. 'I guess you could say I love him. Feel some sort of attachment, anyway. He's my uncle after all. Love is a big word. I mean...' He looked at his hands. 'If you asked me for a list of all the people I love it wouldn't be very long.'

'How long? Four or five?'

'If that. Or two or three. You know who'd be top of the list, don't you?'

He was blushing, really and truly he was blushing. Kelly got up from the sofa and came over to him, kneeling on the floor and resting an arm on his knee. He gave her an awkward smile.

'I love you too, Trav.'

'You don't have to say that.'

'But I just did say it. You heard me, didn't you?'

'You'll think I was fishing.'

'Shut up.'

She pulled his head toward hers and they kissed. Through the French windows came the sound of rain, rain washing the streets and rooftops of Uzès and all the fields and forests around, from Fournhac to Valliguières and beyond. The little river that flowed under the bridge at Fournhac was swollen with the rain, the puddles in the crater in the woods near Valliguières joined up to make bigger puddles. After the kiss Travis said: 'One day we can live at The Vines together. The whole place will be ours. If you want.'

'Your uncle might live to be a hundred. Or he might never die: what if they freeze him?'

Travis laughed. 'I don't think he'd have put me in his Will if freezing would invalidate it. He's eighty-something now ...'

He was interrupted by the ringing of his phone. Kelly reached over to the coffee table and passed it to him. Travis read the number on the display.

'Speak of the devil.'

Kelly got to her feet. She mimed the act of teeth-brushing and Travis nodded. 'Hi, Uncle Harry,' he was saying as she went off to the bathroom. She couldn't hear much of the conversation while she was doing her teeth.

Brush, rinse, spit—water from the tap. She checked her face in the mirror, opened her eyes wide and repositioned a stray hair. When she went back into the room she knew at once that something was wrong. Travis was sitting pale-faced, staring ahead of him, the phone to his ear. Whoever it was was doing a lot of talking.

'You've got to call the police,' he said after a while. 'Call the police and get them to search the place thoroughly. *Thoroughly*, okay? House and gardens. Okay? Do it now, Nico. Get back to me as soon as you know anything.' He hung up.

'What's the matter?'

'Uncle Harry's gone missing. He didn't come down in the morning and when Nico went to check on him his bed hadn't been slept in.'

Kelly sat down on the arm of his chair. 'Your uncle's wandered off somewhere. My great-aunt used to wander off all hours of the day and night. The police would pick her up in her nightie.'

'I've never heard of Uncle Harry doing that. Nico would have said so. He sounded pretty upset on the phone, I thought he was going to break down.'

'He'll turn up, Trav. If he's pushing ninety he's probably got the beginnings of dementia—forgot what he was doing or where he was going. Worst case scenario he's fallen down somewhere and can't get up.'

'I hope you're right.'

'Of course I'm right.'

*

The two strangers were introduced by Max. Julius didn't catch their names, the wall of polyester and rain obscured them, but he shook the men's hands. One of them had a beard and was wearing sunglasses, absurdly, while the other, as tall as Julius but broader in the shoulders, kept transferring his weight from one foot to the other in a sort of dance. Amphetamines perhaps? A tattoo peeped out from the man's coat sleeve, something reptilian and mythic. He probably read fantasy novels.

Philippe had limped over.

'This is just the start, Durward,' he shouted. 'The finished complex will be hundreds of times bigger than that pit. Thousands of trees. If you add up the ages of all the trees which will be chopped down to make way for this governmental wet dream…' He was waving an arm, gesturing at the mechanical digger and the puddles and the duckboards.

'What's your impression, professor?'

Max's voice sounded from close by. Julius turned his head and found himself looking into a pair of brown eyes, excessively bright. The scar on Max's cheek seemed to be mocking him, jeering at him. For some reason he thought of Hugh. I should send a copy of my pamphlet to Hugh, that might placate him. Departmental productivity. Remission of sins.

'Does it take your breath away?' continued Max. 'Are you at a loss for words, professor? Understandable if so. What's being done here is surely too extreme, too revolting for words. Nouns and adjectives are inadequate. And what are words anyway? Sounds that die on the air, marks on paper, shapes on a screen. Whereas this is an insult, a desecration, it demands . . .'

He held up his hand, clenched it into a fist, the platinum ring inches from Julius's chin.

'What does it demand?' asked Julius.

'Well,' said Max, lowering the fist, 'how does that trite old saying go? Actions speak louder than words. Trite but true, don't you think? Return words for words, actions for actions. Meet violence with violence.'

'An eye for an eye.'

'You could put it that way. But it might need to be a hand for an eye, or a head for an eye. To be effective.' He winked.

Julius's phone was ringing. He took it from his pocket, shielding it from the rain with his other hand and bringing it closer to his face. Without any fuss and as if they'd agreed on it beforehand Max deftly relieved him of the phone and passed it to Dany. 'We'll look after that for you,' he said, then beckoned to Laurent. Laurent was at his side and Max was saying something to him, a hand on his arm, the young man nodding. Reptile-tattoo danced from foot to foot. The web of forces connecting the eight figures standing by the crater's rim had subtly altered; there was a shift in the centre of gravity, the range of possibilities seemed to be expanding. Julius felt as if an unseen choreographer were at work.

'What's . . .' he began.

The guy in dark glasses was pointing a gun at him. He's play-acting, thought Julius. I'm meant to be a policeman or a security guard. It's a rehearsal, a demonstration.

'Max, what the hell is this about?' Philippe shouted. He started to move towards the gunman. Reptile-tattoo placed himself in his path. When Philippe attempted to brush him aside he had his arms yanked and held behind his back, the other man grinning and dancing behind him. Eva took a step forward but Dany held up a restraining hand, shaking his head.

'This is Plan B, Philippe,' said Max. His voice was incisive, he didn't need to raise it much to be heard. 'Your Plan A was never going to work. Why would the authorities care what some ageing English academic thinks? You can't fight dogs and guns with blogs and news articles. It wasn't Marx sitting in the British Museum who launched the revolution, it was Lenin, remember?' He folded his arms across his chest, feet planted a little apart. Julius was reminded of Mussolini. 'But your cock-eyed project did lay the groundwork for my own more practicable one, I grant you that. Question: who can put pressure on the French government? Another government. And who can put pressure on that other government?' He looked around as if expecting an answer. 'We can!' he laughed. 'Yes, we can.' Pointing at Julius: 'This English celebrity is worth something, if only to the English. Let me be more precise: the British government would not want the responsibility for his death on their hands. Now would they?'

Tattoo-boy nodded and grinned; it was a great joke, he was enjoying himself immensely.

'A ransom?' asked Philippe. 'You want to get a ransom?'

Max shrugged. 'I'd prefer them to fill in this hole, then to make some undertakings.'

'Which they wouldn't keep.'

'Whereupon we do the same again, kidnap some more people—till they get the idea. They have to know we mean business.' He paused. 'Of course there are other ways of conveying that message. For example…'

He strolled over to the man in dark glasses and placed an index finger on the barrel of the gun. Looking Julius in the face and flicking his upper lip with the tip of his tongue he proceeded to caress the metal barrel back and forth with finger and thumb, eyes half closed now, lascivious and panting…

'*Connard!*' Philippe spat the insult out. Max roared with laughter.

'You're too sensitive, my friend,' he said. 'I was merely imagining a theoretical possibility. It might be as you say, that we settle for money. A lot can be done with half a million euros. You can buy a lot of weaponry.'

'Half a million?' said Julius. He hadn't spoken for a while. Everyone looked at him. The hood of his cagoule was down and his hair and face were wet with rain, the glasses on his beaky nose misted up and the eyes behind them a blur.

'Now don't be modest, professor,' responded Max, 'you surely don't think you're worth any less than that? A famous writer like you?'

Again the explosion of laughter, the open mouth twisting the cheek-scar into a letter V, and all the while the gun pointing at Julius's chest. The guy in the dark glasses stood stock still, he could almost be asleep.

'We shall see what we shall see,' wound up Max. 'All that will be a matter for negotiation. Meanwhile you're both of you our guests. We'll endeavour to make you as comfortable as possible. You'll be taken to one of our places in the country, rather isolated but not without a certain rustic charm—pretty basic facilities, I'm afraid, hot running water and a shared toilet, but you weren't expecting the Ritz, were you. Louis will be looking after you. It may be necessary to make use of blindfolds or handcuffs at various points during your detention, for which I apologise in advance. And now … why not take a last look at the building site you came to inspect, Professor Durward? You too, Philippe. Louis—' he addressed Reptile-tattoo; 'you can let go of him now. You'll have the opportunity of getting to know one another a lot better in due course.'

Philippe's guardian released him and backed off, fidgeting and gurning. Max went over to Laurent who was soon smiling at something he was saying (heads bent in comradely confabulation) so that the scene appeared relaxed, almost domestic, when a sudden darting movement and shouts shattered the picture and Julius saw Reptile-tattoo leaping through the air towards the struggling bodies, Philippe's and the gunman's, the sunglasses knocked off and the nakedness of the face emphasising its anger and surprise, Philippe's hand gripping the other's wrist, the gun now pointing off to the right. '*Run, Julius!*' Philippe's shout acted like an electric shock and Julius pushed past Dany and was running blindly through the trees along the path they had come by with Max's voice flying after him, '*Attrapez-le!*' A shot was fired and he heard someone, Laurent probably, on his trail, footsteps pounding the muddy earth, and there came another shot, followed by a woman's scream. Another scream and then another, and the screaming continued but faded as he got further away from it. The beat of footsteps behind him had stopped abruptly, Laurent must have given up or more likely tripped and fallen, hopefully spraining an ankle, and Julius knew what had happened, knew they had shot Philippe and he saw his bloody head cradled in Eva's lap, the blood pinkening in the rain and their fingers twined for the last time, she sobbing as she had sobbed all those years ago standing in the rain beside the hole, that other hole. Finis, the end, but you have to keep running, you are a wanted man, you are the quarry and the predator is behind you, dogs and men on horseback . . .

Suddenly he was among tents, two grey ones and a dirty green one. He skidded, slowed down, looked for which path to take out of the clearing and upon seeing it started towards it, when a short figure with orange-green hair appeared from behind a tent waving its arms which he had to push to the ground, nearly tripping over the squealing creature. Now he was in among the trees again where it was dark and dense, necessary to go slower, mustn't trip over a root or get tangled in a creeper, and his heart was pounding and his face wet with rain and tears. He could hear his breath heaving and gasping. But they don't seem to be following, do they, the hunt seems to have been called off. To hunt in the rain is a poor business, the dogs quickly lose the scent and one's spirits sink. Another time, they can hunt another time, all such things can be postponed *sine die*, the future is quite empty which is why it is meaningless. Keep going, keep trudging through these damp ferns towards the empty meaningless future. Forwards, forwards! One mustn't turn back, even though behind one there are beckoning ghosts that once were warm, oh Philippe, oh dear old friend your bowels are yet warm though your skin is cold—it ebbs away, the warmth ebbs away, mon vieux. You must have courage. Eva will give you courage.

And here is the edge of the wood and here is the footpath that leads back to Valliguières. The rain is still falling, my shoes are caked in mud and I can hardly see through these glasses but I have the protection of a cagoule, whose hood I have for some reason pulled back. It was so that I might hear better what that man was saying. Let me pull it over my head again, I don't need or wish to hear anything anymore, except the rain of course, always the damn rain, swoosh swish swoosh to the rhythm of my feet. He mentioned half a million euros, why was that again? I forget now. Perhaps it was the cost of the buildings they're going to put up, some sort of research centre, Maia was telling me about it. She sat across the table from me coffee cup in hand and told me all about it. Yes. And now it behoves me to relay the message to the king so that a force might be raised against the invaders, upon whom harsh and condign punishment will fall like a fist of iron. Yes. Those who dishonour the name of Crussol shall live to regret it, and those who wreak havoc in the lands of the Dukes of Uzès shall suffer for it. Their heads shall be stuck on pikes and their entrails fed to the dogs, for they are outlaws and murderers, spreaders of plague and destruction, they have taken a hatchet to Pandora's box and for love of gold and desire of power watch over the deaths of millions.

To his right were muddy allotments, through the grey rain he spotted tomatoes.

In the end we couldn't stop it, Philippe, others might be able to but you and I couldn't, we were armed only with words, your delusion was to think that the hearts of men and women can be wrought upon by written or spoken syllables, as if a wolf or a virus could be persuaded to mend its ways. That was always your delusion.

We weren't armed with words, Durward. You never wrote that pamphlet. Who knows?—we might have succeeded if you had.

But if the goal was so dear to you why didn't you go along with that other man's plan? It was a good plan—frankly it was a much better plan than yours, mon vieux. The cause of Rebex could have received a real boost from my temporary incarceration, you must admit that. And yet you stood in the way, you thwarted the enterprise, you went as far as to let yourself be killed, merely so that an old friend who is already fading from the world should have a little longer in it, should have a stay of execution, though perhaps he himself would reject the bargain. And he does reject it, he rejects it utterly, with bitter angry tears, Philippe, for I would rather have died with you by my side even if it had to be in some farmhouse cellar with a hood over my head and chained to a radiator, do you hear me?

Don't be a fool, Durward. A pointless sacrifice.

And wasn't yours? What about all those who will die in the next pandemic, the Languedoc one? Shouldn't you have thought of them when you were diving towards that gun?

I have thought often of them, you know that. But you were my friend and I was responsible for you. Only the past is real; love and responsibility are forms of relationship with the past. The future must look after itself.

It could be me talking to myself. Those are my ideas, not yours, Philippe. You wouldn't say such a thing.

Have it your own way.

I'm not talking to myself, I absolutely refuse to. It is with Philippe Arentz that I need to come to an understanding, this is a matter which is of intimate concern to both of us, it is very important that we explain ourselves to one another. Everything hangs on that, it may be our last chance to arrive at clarity and consensus. All our conversations have been tending to this goal.

You talk too much.

He was coming into Valliguières, walking past a petrol station on the forecourt of which stood an articulated lorry with *Autodoprava Vodica* written on the side. The driver, pump in hand, stared at him as he passed.

In a few minutes he was approaching the town hall, the mairie. Beyond the town hall the church rose up with its three sturdy pinnacles, the central steeple flanked by spires, and a little further on was a car park in which a solitary white Peugeot sheltered under a plane tree. At a crossroads he spotted a sign for Uzès. Pulling the hood of his cagoule firmly over his head he bent his steps in the direction of the arrow.

I'm going home. Finally I'm going home. There are others I must take leave of, the young man who wants me to do something for a rich uncle, his Australian girl-friend—I need to say goodbye to them all. For the uncle I'm meant to write a lecture, 'How to save the world', or alternatively 'Why bother?', but that's for another occasion, Harry D. Crusoe must wait a little for that, I have various affairs that need attending to first. In my hotel bedroom is a packet of little yellow pills. These I will flush down the toilet. Finis, the end. Then I will go to meet Toni in the Place aux Herbes by the fountain as we agreed. She has suggested we have another child. I will discuss the matter with her. Finally, I will pay a visit to Maia Byrne. She has invited me to Fournhac to view her exhibition of paintings, including one of me seated in her kitchen in Oxford wearing a cravat. I will

*

It had stopped raining some time ago and Kelly and Travis were out walking. They had dined early, in the hotel restaurant: cassoulet, salad Niçoise, a crème brûlée for Travis. The air was fresh and the pavements smelt of rain, and in the evening sky the stars were beginning to come out. People strolled, tourists and residents mingled; the holiday season was winding down and in a couple of weeks autumn would have arrived. In Paris and in other cities cars were being torched and shop windows smashed, protestors clashed with policemen and revolution was in the air, but here in Uzès life went on as normal, urban insanity seemed a long way off.

'Some planes are flying again,' said Travis. 'We should be able to get seats on some flight or other before the end of next week. Then if Uncle Harry hasn't turned up, or the news is bad, I guess I'll have to go over to the states.'

They were standing in the Place du Duché. The little wicket gate was closed and there were no lights on in the windows of the chateau. The duchy was asleep.

'You want me to come with you?'

'It's up to you. I might be having to talk to lawyers and stuff, it could get pretty boring.'

'I'll come.'

Holding hands they moved off, turning left down the Rue Gaston Chauvet.

'What about Julius?' asked Kelly.

'What about him?'

'Do you think you should tell him—I mean, when we see him tomorrow will you mention your uncle? 'Cos of the lecture.'

'If I've heard nothing by tomorrow I'll let him know there might be a problem. Sure. Let's hope I will have heard something.'

They came to the Rue du Dr Blanchard, turned left, then right, proceeded down the Rue de la Calade, going underneath the little stone bridge that spans the narrow street, reached the D5A and crossed over. They were heading for the cathedral. It wasn't long before the church's façade rose up on their left with its vertical lines and circular windows and the two robed figures looking down from their niches and a moment later the Tour Fenestrelle came into view. The pierced stonework was lit up from below and behind it loomed the backdrop of the night sky. Two days earlier they had walked this way with Julius as their guide. He'd told them the history of a murder, a priest's murder.

'Let's sit here for a bit,' said Travis.

They sat down on the bench and Kelly pointed over towards a domed building and said, 'The Racine Pavilion'.

Under the light of a lamp post a man in a cagoule was pacing up and down in front of the pavilion. He would stop and start, now pausing before the stone plaque, now gazing over the low wall which adjoined the building, out towards the wooded horizon. Kelly watched him and felt only mild surprise when the man stood up on the wall, for he probably wanted to get a better view, drink it all in more fully, but then he pulled down the hood of his cagoule and her heart stopped and she whispered 'Trav...'

It is night, the sky bristles with stars. I have been on a long journey. Ghosts are beckoning, I can hear their voices carried to me on the wind: *Come,* they say, *here it is more beautiful—although it is night it is more beautiful, the nights here are more beautiful even than your days…* For I am sick of the day, sick of the sun rising on a bright and empty future when all those whom I love and have loved are nowhere to be found in that brash bright country. Where are they then? They walk in the cool glades of Arcadia or Elysium awaiting my return, Paul and Toni, Maia and Johnny, Philippe, my mother, my father. Below me the trees stand in neat rows, bathed in a dim light, mysterious and expectant. Scented breezes cool my tear-stained cheeks and as I turn my head towards the silhouette of a dome…

Kelly was running. 'Julius!' she cried.

Out of the star-filled canopy a curved segment has been cut: an arch of deeper darkness against the dark velvet of the sky. The child's voice calls again and the black arch shrinks to a point and the stars rush in.

*

Maia woke from a dream. In the dream she and Johnny were walking down the avenue of poplars and he was explaining how he'd just bought a property somewhere and was asking her if she'd join him to start a new life together. 'Where is it?' she asked but he just smiled and winked at her. 'Oh,' she said, knowing now the answer to her own question. 'And can Julius come with us?' Johnny was about to say something when the dream ended and she awoke.

She rubbed her eyes and yawned, then looked over at the clock on the mantelpiece. Ten fifteen. She must have dropped off sitting in her armchair. Perhaps I'll try Julius again, she thought. He didn't answer before. Her phone was on the floor by her feet and she reached down to pick it up. On the other hand... maybe it's a little late—I should perhaps leave it till tomorrow morning. Yes, I'll leave it to tomorrow. Julius might be sleeping. It wouldn't be good to wake him. He needs all the sleep he can get.

Maia got out of her chair and went to the kitchen to make herself some coffee.

ABOUT THE AUTHOR

ROGER TEICHMANN is a writer and philosopher. He teaches at Oxford University and has written several books on philosophy in addition to the two novels *Dog's Twilight* and *The Echo Dies*. He is also a keen musician and has composed music for various forces including a chamber opera, *A Practical Man*. He lives in Oxford.

www.ingramcontent.com/pod-product-compliance
Lightning Source LLC
Chambersburg PA
CBHW030928210726
48290CB00007B/2112